Ransom
By Mail

A Novel by
Paul R. Payton

Dedication

I dedicate this book to my cousin, godfather, and mentor, Martin J. Payton, Jr., because, like the generation before us, you bestowed your love of family and values to me. You took me under your wing and mentored me in business and life. Most of what I've achieved in my adult life finds its direct link back to you. For that I always will be grateful.

Chapter One
Sales Trip

Little Nichole, who was four years old, raced across the family room, her blonde curls bouncing as she headed into the small foyer. She glanced at the travel bag by the door then looked up and asked, "Daddy, are you going away again?"

"Yes, honey," replied her father, "but just for a few days." As Sean swept Nichole into his arms, he asked, "Will you be a good girl for Mommy and help take care of your little sister while I'm away?"

Nichole squeezed her tiny arms around her father's neck. "Yes, Daddy."

Sean lowered her to the floor and tickled her. His wife, Kathryn, came into the foyer with their almost-three-year-old daughter, Lauren, perched on her hip. Seeing her daddy, Lauren stretched out her arms. "Hey, cutie pie," Sean said as he scooped her up and away from Kathryn. "I'm going to miss you guys. How about a big hug and a kiss for Daddy?" After getting his squeeze from Lauren, Sean squatted and picked up Nichole again. He held both his girls, one in each arm. "See ya, honey," he told Kathryn. "I've got to run."

Kathryn leaned in for her own kiss. "Good luck on your trip, and be safe."

Sean lowered his girls to the floor and got in his last tickles. "Thanks. I'll see you when I get back," he said and then headed for his car. As he backed out of the driveway, both of his daughters stood behind the glass storm door, wildly waving goodbye.

Sean worked for ZAP, the pharmaceutical giant, as a salesman. Its large corporate headquarters were located in a quiet suburb just outside Philadelphia. Sean and his family lived close to ZAP's corporate offices, which made it very convenient for him to work both from home and the corporate office when he wasn't on the road making sales calls. Being an outside sales guy meant setting up his own schedule for sales calls and whatever was necessary for entertaining clients. Sean's boss, a tough old Italian guy named Ray, wasn't a stickler for a nine-to-five schedule. He just wanted results. Fortunately, Sean was a producer with consistently good sales figures.

Chapter Two
Watuppa

It wasn't the norm for Sean to travel on a Sunday morning, but one of his clients, a doctor who worked at a medical center in Westchester County, New York, had invited him for a round of golf at the exclusive Watuppa Country Club. Sean was thrilled to have been asked to play with Dr. Tate. It certainly would help with his sales rapport, but more important, being a golfer himself and getting to play on a course that had hosted several US Opens and a couple of PGA events was something Sean had dreamed about since he had caddied at a private country club as a boy.

Sean recalled a comment made years earlier by the famous golf pro Chi Chi Rodriguez. At a US Open match held at Watuppa Country Club, the press asked Chi Chi if he liked playing at that club. Chi Chi replied, "When I was younger, it was my dream just to be able to work at a great course like Watuppa, never mind being able to play here for the US Open title."

Sean drove north from Philadelphia, up through New Jersey, and into New York on I-95. The agenda for the day was to have lunch at the club, play a round of golf, and then have dinner with Dr. Tate and his friends. Next, Sean would drive north toward his old hometown in New England to start the week off on sales calls and then eventually work his way back home on Thursday to Kathryn and the girls.

The traffic on I-95 was unusually brisk this Sunday morning, with even minimal traffic on the George Washington Bridge. A couple of hours flew by, and before Sean knew it, he was pulling into the long driveway entrance of Watuppa Country Club.

The entrance to the club started with a giant stone wall and ornate, wrought iron gates that opened up to the long driveway. The old sycamore trees that lined the drive had grown to form a high canopy over the road. The sycamores, with yellowing autumn leaves mixed with some remaining green leaves, framed Watuppa's gorgeous stone clubhouse ahead on the drive. *Holy shit*, Sean thought. *This is really something else.*

After dropping off his golf clubs at the club's entrance, he parked his car and headed toward the sign for the men's locker room. Once Sean was inside, Dr. Tate greeted him and showed him to his guest locker. "Sean, I'd invite you up here every Sunday if you could promise us a lovely day like today," Dr. Tate told him.

"Yeah, it's a beauty. Thanks so much for inviting me."

Dr. Tate smiled and patted Sean on the shoulder. "Glad to have you."

Dr. Tate was a tall fellow in good shape, considering he was fast approaching his sixties. His hair showed more signs of aging than his physical being. The hair that once had been curly and brown was starting to thin on top and looked more gray than brown. Other than that, someone might take Dr. Tate for a man in his mid-forties. "Leave your gear in the locker, and let's go upstairs to the grill room for some lunch and to meet the other guys."

Sean smiled. "Sounds good to me."

Upstairs in the men's grillroom, two other Watuppa Country Club members were waiting for Sean and Dr. Tate. Dr. Bean was an associate of Dr. Tate's, while Jim Winslow was a younger fellow, closer to Sean's age. Jim was Dr. Tate's neighbor and lived just down the road from the doctor's home, which was located on the course's seventeenth hole.

The grillroom was exquisite, with a classic large mahogany bar. The back of the bar was lined with mirrors that extended almost to the ceiling and were at least fourteen feet high. Framed photos of golf's greatest players, who at one time or another had played at Watuppa, graced the walls. Sean spotted a classic photo of Jack Nicklaus with his arm looped over the shoulder of Arnie Palmer. The photo showed both men smiling as they walked up Watuppa's famed par five, the eighteenth hole at the 1967 US Open. Golf history abounded everywhere Sean looked.

"Guys, this is my friend, Sean Murphy," Dr. Tate said.

Dr. Bean reached up to shake Sean's hand. "Is this your first time playing at Watuppa?"

"Yes, and I'm truly looking forward to it."

"Well," Jim said, "you certainly picked a beautiful day to come."

Lunch was perfect. *That was probably the best Reuben sandwich I've ever had*, Sean thought. After the meal, the men headed out to play. The first tee was just as Sean had remembered it from watching the tournaments on TV. It was a par four, with a slight fade to the left, 386 yards, and had deep bunker trouble on three sides of the green.

"Show us the way, Sean," Dr. Tate spouted.

Taking a deep breath to calm the butterflies in his stomach, Sean teed up and smacked a decent drive, slicing it just a bit but remaining in the fairway and needing only a four- or five-iron to reach the green. *Whew!* Sean thought. *Boy, am I happy to have hit the ball decently enough not to embarrass myself on the first tee.*

The round of golf was going along great, with the team of Dr. Tate and Sean one up on the seventeenth hole. They were winning a bet they had placed against Dr. Bean and Jim. "Two holes to go, and you're one down," declared Dr. Tate. "Do you fellows wish to give us a press?"

"Do you mean an extra bet so we can get even?" asked Dr. Bean.

"Sure. Why not?" said Dr. Tate. "The last time I pressed you, you folded like a lawn chair."

Everyone laughed at the little jab. As the fellows walked up the lush seventeenth fairway, Dr. Tate gestured to one of the large homes. "That's my house on the left there, and the next house farther down the fairway, closer to the green, is Jim's."

The size and grandeur of both homes impressed Sean. Similar in style, all the houses in the area were stone with slate shingles, copper gutters, and huge cut-glass windows that overlooked the course. Each home had a large back patio for sitting out and entertaining. The landscaping at both Dr. Tate's home and Jim's home was mature, with some English ivy growing on the north sides of the houses, making them look much like buildings on an Ivy League campus or an old English estate.

"Wow! Your house is gorgeous, and Jim's house is too." Sean paused, staring into the distance, past the homes. "What did you say Jim does for a living?"

"He works for the brokerage house of Winslow and McClure on Wall Street."

"So Jim is the Winslow of Winslow and McClure?"

"Not quite," said Dr. Tate. "Jim's grandfather started the firm many years ago, and Jim's dad is the president and CEO of the company. Young Jim here does pretty well and is probably the heir apparent, but his father makes him move up the ladder one step at a time."

"I figured he had to be doing pretty damn good to be a member at Watuppa and have a house on the course," said Sean.

Dr. Tate told Sean that the house originally belonged to Jim's parents' but that they had moved into a penthouse apartment in Manhattan that overlooked the East River. He added that they had a second home in the Hamptons.

Sean dropped the conversation about the Winslows. He remembered his own father telling him about how he had lost most of his retirement money through the Winslow and McClure brokerage house after one of their brokers had convinced him to move most of his money into an oil company stock called Enron, which later tanked and went bankrupt; after that several corporate officers were sentenced to prison for cooking the books. The dollar amount Sean's father lost wasn't much compared to what some investors lost, but it was nearly twenty years' worth of his bricklayer's pension. Sean thought that just wasn't fair. His dad had spent his life working and saving for his retirement only to lose most of it on advice given by the folks at Winslow and McClure. *Hell,* Sean thought. *It didn't much matter to the firm. They would still make their money on the buy and the sell, no matter which way the stock went.*

Sean's dad had since passed away, but Sean knew this matter was something his father had fretted about often. His dad would say, "It wasn't fair!" Sean's feelings were much the same as his father's. It really wasn't fair; in fact it was a very bad deal.

Dr. Bean and Jim won the seventeenth hole, putting the match even and themselves one up on the press bet. "I told you that you'd fold under the pressure," Dr. Bean said.

Dr. Tate replied, "That's why I brought Sean. He'll save my butt."

Sean was the last to tee off, and as luck would have it, he hit a good ball right down the middle of the fairway. Dr. Tate's ball was in big-time trouble in the tall rough, and he also would have some problems with trees. His decision to lose a shot and just chip back out to the fairway was an easy one. Like Sean, Dr. Bean and Jim were in good shape.

Dr. Bean and Jim had decent second shots, and both hit their third shots to the green, having putts of close to twenty feet. Dr. Tate was still a basket case and was going from bad to worse. He arrived on the green in five. Sean's third shot was great, landing eight or nine feet from the pin. "Well, it's up to you, partner," called Dr. Tate.

"Great," Sean muttered sarcastically.

Dr. Bean, being the farthest away, putted first and missed the hole, but he tapped it in for par. "Let her rip, Jim," he shouted to his partner. "You've got nothing to lose."

Jim lined up his putt and hit the ball. They all watched it roll dead into the cup for a birdie. With a whoop and a holler, Dr. Bean and Jim were doing a premature victory dance.

Dr. Tate called over to Sean, "Okay, guy, knock it into the hole, and shut these two up."

Sean lined up his putt and tapped the ball, sending it rolling just past the outside edge of the hole. Close, but no cigar. Jim and Dr. Bean again whooped it up with joy in their victory.

Jim smiled. "We were one down with two to go, and we pulled it off. You guys now owe us two ways."

"Sorry, Dr. Tate," Sean said.

"That's okay," Dr. Tate told him. "We'll get these bastards another time in a rematch. In the meantime, let's head over to the clubhouse for a drink and some dinner."

In the clubhouse, the usual banter of busting balls and reliving good shots went on. Sean was having a great time, but inside he knew he would always be only just a guest. It seemed to him that his caste in life was to be middle of the road with a decent life, but he never would be in a position to be one of these "special people."

The dinner was just as great as Sean had expected. He thanked his host and the other men but said he needed to get a move on. "Relax," Dr. Tate said. "We're going over to my house for a quick drink. You can follow me over there, have one for the road, and then be on your way. Where are you going again?"

"Up to New England, to my old hometown in Fall River, Massachusetts. From there I'll make sales calls and then work my way back down to Philadelphia by Thursday."

Dr. Bean interrupted. "Hey, isn't Fall River where Lizzy Borden killed her parents?"

"Yes," Sean replied, then quoted the famous rhyme. "Lizzy Borden had an axe, gave her mother forty whacks. When she saw what she had done, she gave her father forty-one."

"Yeah, that's the one," said Dr. Bean. "You grew up there?"

"I lived there until I went off to college and for a couple of years after that. Fall River is a tough old mill town, lots of unemployment and lots of crime. That's why I chose to live outside of Philadelphia."

Jim chimed in, "Hell, Philly is no garden spot when it comes to crime."

"You're right," Sean said, "but I live just far enough outside the city where we don't have much of a problem in that department."

"Do you still have family in Massachusetts?" Dr. Tate asked.

"Yes, but most of my relatives have passed away, including my mom and dad. All I have now are an aunt and a cousin who are still Mass-holes."

"Mass-holes! That's pretty good." Dr. Bean laughed. "I'll have to remember that for one of my Bostonian friends."

Sean followed Dr. Tate from the clubhouse to Dr. Tate's home. As he pulled off the street to Dr. Tate's fully landscaped driveway and up to the big circular drive, he thought, *Wow, this is even more incredible looking from the front than it was from the course.* As Sean exited his car, Dr. Bean and Jim Winslow pulled up behind him.

"Quite the place," Dr. Bean said to Sean as they walked toward the house.

"It sure is. I can hardly wait to see the inside."

"Come on in," Dr. Tate called out.

Sean and the guys entered Dr. Tate's house with Sean in total awe. "Sure is a beautiful home you have," Sean said. Dr. Tate smiled and thanked him for his comment.

"Come on in to my favorite room, the golf room." Dr. Tate led them into a grand room, which featured a gorgeous bar, leather couches and chairs, and loads of golf memorabilia.

At the back end of the room, Sean could see the seventeenth fairway through the large cut-glass windows. "Quite the view you have, Doc," he said.

"Thank you. The best view is from Jim's house. Jim can see the fairway and up to the seventeenth green. Look here." Dr. Tate motioned Sean to come closer to the window.

Because the leaves on the trees were beginning to fall, Sean could see through most of the wooded area that separated the houses, and he saw most of Jim Winslow's home. "I see what you mean. Jim, you also have a gorgeous home," Sean said.

"Thanks," Jim said. "I'd take you over there right now, but the house is a wreck. My wife, Molly, and I are having our first baby this month, and she's having the spare bedroom turned into a nursery. I'm lucky to have gotten a pass to play golf today."

Dr. Bean chirped in. "Let's have a toast to the new baby you're about to have!"

"Here, here!" said Dr. Tate, as he handed beers to the guys. Sean asked Jim whether he knew what gender their baby was going to be, and Jim said it was going to be a boy.

"Congratulations!" said Sean. "My wife and I have two little girls. We're debating going for one more to see if we can't get lucky and have a boy."

"That would be nice," said Jim. "We'll probably have another child or maybe two more, depending on whether the second one is a girl."

As Sean lifted his beer to drink his last swig, he held it forward to Jim. "Best of luck with the baby to you and your wife."

"Thanks," said Jim.

Sean again thanked everyone for a fabulous day, bid his farewells, and began his drive up to Fall River.

Chapter Three
Daydreaming

As Sean drove north, he thought about the terrific day he'd had and what it must be like to be one of the lucky "special people." He imagined what it would be like to have been born into such wealth, with the big homes, clubs, vacations, all the best clothes, jewelry, and dining at fancy restaurants. He also imagined what it must be like not to worry about money, mortgages, car payments, college tuition for the kids, and retirement. *God*, Sean thought. *Why couldn't that have been me?*

As he drove into the night, his thoughts drifted to a movie he and Kathryn recently had watched called *Ransom*. The film, which starred Mel Gibson, was about a corporate mega millionaire whose child is kidnapped. Mel Gibson's character pulls a reversal on the kidnappers by telling them that instead of giving them the large amount of money they demand, he would use that money and more to find them if they didn't immediately return his child. Of course, in the movie, the kidnappers get caught, and the star gets his child. Sean's thoughts wandered further. What if someone were to kidnap the Winslow baby boy, the new heir to the Winslow name, business, and fortune?

Maybe because there was nothing else to do while driving, or just for the purpose of killing time, Sean continued to think about how someone might kidnap the Winslow baby and not get caught. As he drove closer to his destination, the thoughts persisted, sending him all kinds of scenarios about how such a crime could be pulled off. It seemed silly to be thinking this way, but his mind was occupied with the prospect that such a crime could be successfully committed if planned carefully. With all the daydreaming involving his kidnap scenario, the drive passed quickly, and before Sean knew it, he was driving over the Taunton River on the Braga Bridge, headed into Fall River, Massachusetts.

From the bridge, he saw the lights from the older tenement homes that were built to stack as many millworkers as close to the textile mills as possible. The glory days of this mill town were long gone, with the textile mills moving down south, closer to the cotton fields in the early 1900s. What was left was just another tough New England mill town with higher than average unemployment.

For the average blue-collar worker in the trades, it was difficult to continually have steady work. That's why the memory of Sean's father having lost most of his bricklayer's pension stung a bit earlier that day when he had heard the corporate name of Winslow and McClure.

As Sean took the exit into the heart of the town, he thought, *Great, it's still early. I'll call Kathryn to let her know all went well, then I'll hit a couple of the old hot spots. There's always a chance I'll run into an old flame and get lucky.*

At the hotel, Sean dialed home, and after a short ring, he heard Kathryn's response. "Hello."

"Hi, honey."

"Hi! How was your day? Did you play well?"

"Yeah. I actually played pretty good." Sean paused for a moment. "The course and clubhouse are unreal, and Dr. Tate's house is amazing."

"Did you play with anyone else?"

"No one special. Just two other members who know Dr. Tate." Sean realized he had just lied to his wife in neglecting to mention Jim Winslow. Was this the initiation of a plan? Was the longest journey now starting with the first step, a little lie—or in Sean's case, a lie by omission? After recounting the rest of his day and asking about the girls, he said good night to Kathryn and hung up.

Chapter Four
The Belmont

Sean's first stop in Fall River was a neighborhood bar called the Belmont. It was actually a house, with the first floor functioning as the bar. This downtown bar had a diverse clientele, from lawyers and politicians to guys from the trades. It also had quite a few ladies who stopped in for after-work drinks. Sean's father used to frequent the place, and it was Sean's favorite haunt when he returned to his old turf.

When Sean walked in, he noticed the bar wasn't too crowded, and he got a big greeting from the bartender, Eddie P. "Hey, look who's back in town!" Eddie loudly informed the patrons at the bar. Acknowledging the "welcome back home" gesture, Sean offered him a broad smile and leaned over the bar to shake one of Eddie's big paws. "Hey, your usual?" Eddie asked.

"Yeah, and give Donnie and Michael a drink," Sean said as he walked toward the end of the bar. The two men greeted him with firm handshakes and a few pats on the back and in unison chimed in, "Good to see you, Sean."

"You too. Cheers!" Sean tipped the top of his beer bottle to theirs. The three men had known one another since third grade at St. Joseph's Elementary.

"Well, what's going on with you? Has your wife thrown your sorry ass out of the house yet?" asked Donnie, and they all laughed.

"Not yet. I'm an angel at home," Sean commented.

Michael felt his beer almost come out his nose, and all of them busted up again. When he finished laughing and wiping his nose and eyes on his sleeve, he said, "You really must have her fooled."

"Yeah, that's why I never bring her up here. So what have you guys been up to?"

"Oh, you know, same old, same old," Donnie said. "Nothing up here changes too much."

After a couple of beers and a bit of reminiscing, Sean said, "Say, does Shirley still tend bar at the Mo' Bar?"

"Yeah, but I don't know if she works on the weekends. Why? Are you still tapping that?" Donnie asked.

Sean shook his head. "No, I haven't seen her in years but wouldn't mind bumping into her tonight."

"Bumping into her?" Michael raised an eyebrow and gave Sean a sheepish grin, and the three erupted in laughter again.

Sean bid farewell to his friends. Donnie, pointing the tip of his bottle directly at him said, "You may have them all fooled down there in the land of Brotherly Love, but up here we still know who you are."

Sean gave the men a big smile, a wink, and a wave and headed out the door on his way to check out the Mo' Bar. Perhaps a certain barmaid would be working that night.

Chapter Five
The First Step

The next morning, Sean was off to a meeting in Providence, Rhode Island, to make a presentation to a few doctors about ZAP's new anti-inflammatory drug, Tilamax. The drug was still a year or so away from medical testing and FDA approval, but ZAP's marketing plan was to start planting seeds early about the new product, keeping the medical community apprised about its positive test results along the way until final approval came from the FDA.

From all that Sean was privy to, he could see this new drug was what he was touting it to be, and around the time the drug would be coming out, there wouldn't be a baby boomer that wouldn't have a use for it. He knew Tilamax was one of the major products ZAP was looking to for huge future profits. *Perhaps now's the time to purchase more stock in ZAP,* he thought. *If I wait until the drug gets closer to FDA approval, the bloody stock will already be up in price, but shit, where the hell am I going to get any decent amount of money to buy the stock or even just some extra cash to help make life a bit easier? A day late and a dollar short again. I'm never going to catch a break. It'll be Dr. Tate, who'll tell his stockbroker friend, Jim Winslow, about the new product, and they'll be the ones with the means to capitalize on ZAP's stock and make the really big bread. Yeah, the same guys who screwed my dad will score again.*

* * *

On Thursday, Sean had worked his way into southern Connecticut. Between each sales call presentation, he was plagued by the recurring thoughts of the kidnapping plot he had dreamed up while driving to New England. By the time he headed back to New York, he felt compelled again to drive to Watuppa Country Club, and for curiosity's sake, just kind of look around.

Once again, Sean drove through the club's giant ornate wrought iron gate. This time, the goose bumps he had felt last Sunday were replaced with a surge of adrenaline and excitement. *What the hell is happening to me?* he thought.

Right before Watuppa's clubhouse, the main drive forked off to the left with a sign that indicated the road was for deliveries. Sean took the left fork toward the delivery entrance then turned left again to another sign that pointed to the maintenance buildings. As he slowly drove down the drive, he noticed a few small parking areas, where workers or subcontractors could park, just shy of the large maintenance building. Sean pulled into the closest parking area and parked his car.

After surveying the area, he exited his car and took a little walk toward the edge of the tree line that separated the course from the maintenance buildings. As he continued his walk, he noticed that he could see Jim Winslow's house through the brush and trees on the seventeenth hole. Curious to see more, he explored the area and was pleased to find that large, overgrown laurel bushes stood between the rows of mature oaks and sycamores. He realized he could stand in the bushes and not be seen at all. Sean moved into the bushes and found that before he gave up his cover, he was probably within a hundred yards of the back side of Jim Winslow's back patio. *Wow*, he thought. *If someone were to kidnap the Winslows' baby, this is certainly where he'd do it from.*

As Sean left the Watuppa Country Club, he hit the trip meter on his odometer to see how far of a drive it was to the exit back to I-95 south. Keeping one eye on the road and the other on the odometer, he checked the distances. It was .4 miles from the first maintenance building parking area to the entrance gate. Taking a left onto Gwynedd Drive, he went another 1.1 miles to a road without a sign—the road to the interstate exit—and it ended up being .7 miles. The total driving distance to the interstate exit was only 2.2 miles and took just under four minutes.

During his drive home, Sean again was occupied with thoughts about how he could kidnap the Winslow baby after he was born. Could it be done, and could he accomplish such a ludicrous scheme without being caught and with no one getting hurt?

Chapter Six
Justification

First Sean had to justify in his own mind why he would take such a crazy risk. If he were to get caught, he might spend the rest of his life in prison. His wife, Kathryn, and his two girls, Lauren and Nichole, would be devastated, and their lives would be ruined. The idea didn't make any sense at all, but Sean kept thinking about it.

He also thought about the trauma the kidnapping would cause the Winslows. Hell, they hadn't done anything to him, but then again, how many pensions or savings like his dad's had been lost? How many lives were affected by the corporate greed of Winslow and McClure to make huge profits by pushing stocks they knew were dogs, just to make a commission? Also, the profit Jim and Dr. Tate probably would make on Tilamax would probably more than cover any ransom demand he would ever ask for.

What would be the amount to ask for? And just how much could Sean spend a year in cash without sending red flags to the IRS or other agencies that watch cash transactions? These questions flowed in and out of Sean's mind.

Sean thought that if someone had, let's say, one million dollars, how could he spend it? How could he make the money clean? How do bookies and drug dealers do it? Sean had some thoughts on this, but it still seemed like millions of unknown questions needed to be answered. Another thought that popped into Sean's head was the FBI's investigation. Their textbook profile for the perpetrator of this sort of crime wouldn't be a college-educated married man with two children, a decent job, and a home. That wouldn't make sense to anyone. *Shit*, he thought. *All this is actually to my advantage.* With that thought, the wheel of fortune kept right on spinning.

Chapter Seven
The Clean Room

When Sean opened the door to his house, the smell from the kitchen told him that Kathryn was cooking meatloaf. Good—he was hungry. The thud of his bags hitting the floor and the door closing behind him created the alert for the girls to come running to greet their father.

"Hey, my gorgeous cuties! Daddy missed you." The standing ritual of tickles and Sean falling to the floor, acting like a jungle gym for the girls, went on until Kathryn called out that dinner was ready. "Come on, guys," Sean said. "Mommy's calling us."

With both girls holding onto his legs, Sean approached Kathryn and leaned forward to give her a big hug and kiss. "Hi, toots. I missed you."

Kathryn replied, "Missed you too, honey. You timed your arrival just in time for dinner."

"Yeah. I got lucky. Traffic was pretty good today. I'm starved."

That night, after the girls were put to bed, Sean poured himself and Kathryn two big glasses of wine. "Hey! Not too much," Katherine said. "I'll be looped."

Sean smiled. "Well, maybe that's part of my plan."

Kathryn reached for her glass and took the first sip. "I've got a good idea what your plan is, and I don't need this big a glass of wine to be part of it."

* * *

When the weekend came, Kathryn was shocked to find Sean cleaning the basement. "What the heck has gotten into you?" she asked.

"I just felt like consolidating things and creating a bit more storage space. I also could use a place to do my sales reports and stuff. You know I can't get anything done upstairs when the girls are around."

"Do I get a spot down here too?"

"No such luck, honey. You'll have to stay upstairs in the combat zone. Speaking of those little hooligans, what are they up to now?"

"I've got them taking a nap. Feel like taking a quick nap with me?"

"You know…" Sean grinned. "I believe I can put this basement project on hold for maybe an hour."

Kathryn laughed. "What do you want to do with the remaining fifty-seven minutes?"

After the so-called nap with Kathryn, Sean spent the rest of the afternoon in the basement, sorting out an area for what he called his "clean room." The preparations for the possible kidnapping and ransom exchange would be done there. *If this kidnapping is to be done,* he thought, *I need to have everything thoroughly thought out. My plan must be absolutely perfect, and if anything, anything at all, seems not to work, I'll simply abort.*

Sean repeated these thoughts until they actually made sense to him. *Hell,* he told himself. *I'll plan everything for the kidnapping, and if anything doesn't seem right, I'll just stop, cancel the plan, and go back to my life with nobody getting hurt.* The mantra of these thoughts now seemed rational to Sean, and his preparations began.

In his new clean room, he had an old wooden desk with drawers that could lock. This would be good, as he didn't need anyone finding out what he was doing. Kathryn wasn't a snoop, but he didn't want her accidentally coming across any evidence. After removing several bags of clutter and stacking boxes, he had set up a neat area for his office. Before going back upstairs, he sat down to write out his initial plan with questions and answers. To have the perfect plan, he'd have to do a good amount of due diligence. He picked up a pen and jotted down a series of notes and questions.

Chapter Eight
The Plan

Sean's plan would be different. Most kidnappings start with the abduction, move to the demand for the ransom, and finally permit the exchange of the person kidnapped for the ransom money. This is usually done with several phone conversations to the party paying the ransom or to the FBI, who are involved in helping the family of the kidnapped individual. The family usually has some demands of their own, such as proof of life, a quick "Are you okay?" phone call to the kidnapped person, and being able to negotiate the terms of the deal.

There are also the usual law enforcement tactics, such as tracing the calls, marking the ransom money, and staking out the exchange location. Also, new advancements in criminal forensics meant the FBI would trace every piece of evidence to find any link to the kidnapper. The FBI would interview everyone associated with the Winslows—friends, family, employees, business associates, members of Watuppa Country Club, visitors to their house, etc. Even with all that, Sean thought his plan was unique and that if he stuck to it, it could work.

To begin with, he would have to figure out how to successfully kidnap the baby, unseen, and get away clean. His initial plan was to use the Watuppa Country Club as the starting point, where he could seize the baby and make a clean exit to I-95. Since Watuppa's seventeenth hole backed up to the Winslows' backyard, offering easy access from the workers' entrance with trees and bushes for cover, Sean could conduct surveillance of what was going on in the Winslow household and look for any openings to snatch the baby.

Next would be the communications for the ransom. *If I never talk with the Winslows or the FBI, they can't make any demands of me,* Sean thought. *My communication will be one sided, as my only correspondence to them will be through the US mail. Most kidnappers want the money right away. There will be no rush with my plan. I'll take my time until I'm sure everything is exactly how I want it to be. I'll communicate with them on a regular basis, assuring the Winslows that no harm will come to their baby. But I'll tell them that if they don't pay the ransom and don't follow my instructions, they'll never see their baby again. The baby will simply be raised by someone else.*

Sean was also sure that because of his planned, steady communications, including photos of the baby and constant reassurance that no harm would come to the child, the baby's mother eventually would pressure her husband and family to stop listening to the FBI and go along with Sean's plan. He felt that, given time, Mrs. Winslow would begin to trust him. This would be the hub of his entire kidnapping plan.

Sean also had some thoughts regarding how to recover the ransom money without the FBI capturing him. First he would receive the ransom money, and after he was sure everything was okay, he would return the baby. This is where the baby's mother trusting him would have to work. If Sean felt the baby's mother trusted him to return the baby only after he had the ransom money, he'd be pretty much home free.

Other crucial questions entered Sean's mind. *If I were to successfully kidnap the baby, then what?* he wondered. *How do I bring home a baby boy to Kathryn? How would I explain that to her? It could take months before I felt it was the right time to collect the ransom money.* Sean twirled a pencil as his mind wandered. *How do I keep Kathryn from hearing about the kidnapping? She occasionally watches the news on TV, reads the newspaper, and goes to the store. Even if by some miracle she didn't suspect anything, the neighbors might.* He had sort of an idea regarding this problem, but he'd have to think more about it. *Well, I have a lot to figure out, but I also have several months to think about things and to prepare. Start organizing all your thoughts and make all the preparations now,* he told himself.

With that last thought, Sean heard Kathryn call down the basement stairs, "Hey, cellar dweller, dinner's ready. Come on up."

Sean shouted up the stairs, "Be right up, hon." He put the notepad into the desk drawer and turned the lock shut.

Chapter Nine
The Delivery

Halloween was a big day at the Murphy household. The entire neighborhood was decorated with pumpkins, cornstalks, witches, and ghosts. Lauren and Nichole, decked out in their costumes, were very excited. Lauren's costume was that of a little monkey. The only part of her showing was the round circle of her face with her blackened nose. The rest of the costume was brown and had a neat tail, with a tan, round belly. She couldn't have been any more loveable. Nichole chose to be a fairy princess with wings and a magic wand and looked just as adorable.

Kathryn walked the neighborhood with the girls, watching them go up to all the houses to trick-or-treat. Sean stayed home, dishing out candy to the neighborhood children. There were so many that after the girls came home with their candy, Sean had to steal a little to give out to the remaining trick-or-treaters.

"How many kids are there in this neighborhood?" he asked Kathryn.

I don't know, but the streets are full of children. I think some parents bring their kids to this neighborhood because there are so many families and the homes are so well decorated."

"That must be the case. We never ran out of candy before."

* * *

At the Winslow home, few visitors came trick-or-treating. Although the houses were decorated to some degree, it was an older residential area. Also, Halloween was the due date for Jim's wife, Molly. At this point, she looked as though she may have swallowed one of the pumpkins they had on display outside their front door. As she walked, she waddled. Earlier that day, Molly had gone to her doctor to see how well she was coming along. While Molly was being examined, her gynecologist said it could be any time now.

Molly had told her doctor, "I want the baby out now, but I don't want him born on Halloween."

The doctor chuckled. "Go home and relax," she said. "It still may be today. If it's not today, for sure it'll be tomorrow. Give me a call when your water breaks or if your contractions are two minutes apart."

The next morning, Molly was in the bathroom, putting on her makeup. Suddenly she called out, "Jim, better call Dr. Colleen. My water just broke, and I'm feeling contractions."

Jim rushed into the room and asked if she was okay.

"I'm fine, but it's time to go to the hospital."

"Okay." Jim gave her a smile that lit up the room. "Hey, hey!" he shouted. "I'm going to be a dad!" Then he added, "I'll grab your overnight bag and get the car ready."

"Okay, Mr. Daddy. I'll be right down."

With the hospital about five minutes away, there was no sweat in arriving on time, and Dr. Colleen was already at the hospital.

Several hours later, Molly was pushing, with her face flushed red and beads of sweat on her forehead. Jim stood next to her, offering encouragement. One last push, with Molly's breathing like a choo-choo train, and soon the doctor was smiling as she guided out the baby. "Congratulations!" she announced. "You have a beautiful, healthy-looking boy."

Jim was elated. This was the best day of his life. He had a son—his baby boy. No father on Earth could have been happier. Molly had tears of joy in the corners of her eyes as the nurse passed her the baby to hold. "Oh, my God," Molly said. "He's so cute. Look, Jim." She turned the baby so Jim could see him. "He's a Winslow. Look at his blue eyes and fuzzy blond hair."

Jim was already on his cell phone, texting the news of the birth of their son to his parents and then to Molly's mom and dad. This was certainly a joyous day for Jim, Molly, and their families.

Chapter Ten
Sand Through the Hourglass

Over the next few months, Sean traveled several times back up to New England on business. Each time he drove up the Atlantic coast, he'd stop by the Watuppa Country Club. It seemed only like yesterday when he had first come to play golf at Watuppa. In autumn New England had been in its full glory, with its foliage of bright yellows, tans, and reds. Now the leaves had all but disappeared into the gloomy grayness of winter. The giant sycamores and oaks that lined the entrance of Watuppa and its fairways were now barren, making it very easy to see through the wood-lined paths that bordered the fairways to the estate homes on the course.

Sean pulled off the main entrance that led to the clubhouse. As he pulled up to the first parking lot, he clearly saw the back of the Winslow home. He exited his car and zipped up his jacket. "Geez, it's cold," he muttered. He moved slowly toward the woods that separated the course from Jim Winslow's estate. Approaching the woods, he looked behind him to see whether anyone was around. *No one. Good*, thought Sean. He looked farther down the course, toward the sound of leaf blowers and tractors to see workers clearing the course of remaining leaves. The workers were in the distance and seemed too preoccupied with what they were doing to notice anything unusual about Sean walking near the woods. Besides, it would be typical for residents of neighboring homes to go for walks around the course. Sean was sure the workers were used to seeing this, as he recalled some ladies walking the cart path the day he had played golf there.

Once into the woods, Sean moved up to the last laurel bush that gave him good cover. He estimated the distance to the back of the Winslows' house to be seventy to eighty yards, maximum. All seemed quiet around the home, with the patio furniture covered up and tucked away. Burlap had been wrapped around the shrubs to protect them from the sometimes harsh, freezing winter winds. Sean remained there only a minute or two, etching the landscape into his mind before returning to his car and heading back down I-95 to travel home to Kathryn and the girls.

As he crossed the Delaware River from the New Jersey Turnpike, he entered the Pennsylvania Turnpike on the other side of the bridge. After picking up his toll ticket, he had an epiphany, discovering the missing pieces in his puzzle. "Yes," he said joyously, tapping his steering wheel. "Yes. This will work."

Chapter Eleven
Pieces in the Puzzle

Back in Fall River, Sean had an aunt from his mother's side, who was sort of the black sheep of the family. Sean's Aunt Phyllis never did anything that would cause the family to disown her; it was just that she never seemed to fit in anywhere.

Sean remembered that they never went to Aunt Phyllis's house when he was growing up. His mom would say, "It's always filthy. My mother would roll over in her grave if she could see how Phyllis keeps her house." The only time he'd ever see or hear from Aunt Phyllis would be for a family wedding or a funeral.

Aunt Phyllis had just one child, a daughter named Nancy. She was Sean's younger cousin and was twenty-three years old. Occasionally, when Sean was up in Fall River, he'd visit old friends at some of the local pubs. From time to time, he'd run into his cousin. Sean once had described Nancy to Kathryn as "your typical mill town tramp."

Nancy had had numerous bouts with drugs, booze, and loser guys, and even at her young age, one could plainly see the wear and tear in her face. Sean never held any of Nancy's problems against her, as he knew all too well how tough it was to grow up in Fall River. Hell, if it hadn't have been for an uncle of his personally knowing a judge, Sean himself may have ended up in jail on a breaking-and-entering charge. As a result of his uncle's influence, however, Sean received a six-month suspended sentence without adjudication, and because he kept his nose clean during those six months, there was no permanent record listed.

Nancy and her mother never did get along. No one remembered or cared where Nancy's dad had run off to. Whenever Sean ran into Nancy, he'd greet her warmly, buy her a couple of drinks, and reminisce about happier family times when they were younger. When he was leaving, he'd slip her a twenty-dollar bill. When he returned from his New England trips, Sean would mention to Kathryn that he had run into Nancy. "Oh, that poor dear," his wife would say. "It seems like she never had a chance."

Chapter Twelve
Planting the Seed

Sean pulled into his driveway, grabbed his travel bag and briefcase from the trunk, and made his way to the front door. As soon as he shouted his greeting, he heard little squeals, and thundering feet came running.

"Hey, guys." He bent down to his knees to look at Lauren and Nichole. "If Mommy tells me you were good while I was away, I've got a present for both of you." Both of the girls' heads nodded, with Nichole jumping up and down declaring that indeed she had been good. "Okay," Sean said. "Let's go see what Mommy has to say about that."

Sean embraced Kathryn with a deep "I missed you" kiss. "Wow," she said. "Who are you, and what have you done to my husband?"

"Hey," Sean said. "I just missed you. That's all."

"Then come here and do it again."

Sean looped his arm around her back and over to her shoulder. He pulled her closer and tilted her head slightly backward. "Hmmmm," Kathryn said as Sean laid his most passionate kiss on her and held her in the position for an extended moment or two. As he released her, she shouted, "Okay, kids. It's bedtime." The girls jumped up and down and loudly protested. "I know, I know," she told them. "Mommy was just kidding."

Nichole said, "Tell Daddy I was good."

"Yes, dear. Both Nichole and Lauren were very good and helped Mommy all week."

"Well, then," Sean said, "after dinner I'll give you two your gift. Now, skedaddle. Go to the playroom, and let Mommy and Daddy have a little time to talk." With the promise of a present after dinner, the girls retreated to their playroom.

Sean said to Kathryn, "Guess who I ran into up in Fall River?"

"Who?"

"My cousin, Nancy."

"Oh? How is she?"

"Same old, same old, with the exception that she's now a mom."

"No way. She got married?"

"I didn't say that."

"Oh. I should have figured. What did she have?"

"A cute little baby boy. I ran into her with the baby at the supermarket while I was picking up some Portuguese chourico and linguica for us. Then I went over to Nancy's dumpy little welfare apartment on the third floor and spent a little time with her. I bought her a load of diapers, baby food, and stuff—gifts from you and me."

"That was nice of you."

Sean nodded. "Yeah, I thought it was better to buy all the stuff for the baby than to just give Nancy some money. Even though she seems a bit better, she might use the cash for booze or something and not for the baby."

"You're right. You made a good move. How old is the baby?"

Sean quickly estimated how old the Winslow baby would be, figuring he was probably born in late October or early November. "About three to four months. I'm not sure."

"What's the baby's name?"

"Ryan. God, you know, it's tough enough growing up in that bloody city with good parents, never mind a single parent with drug and booze problems."

"Oh, I know," Kathryn said. "I'll say a prayer for Nancy that things work out for her and the baby."

Sean smiled inside, thinking, *Great. That seed has now been planted.*

Chapter Thirteen
Due Diligence

Later that weekend, down in the clean room, Sean reviewed the checklist of items he eventually would need. He knew that communicating through letters meant he would need to type them. Since computers hold memory, even if deleted, he decided he'd use old typewriters. They were cheap enough, and although they could be traced forensically, they were easily disposable. He would collect a number of older typewriters, and after every couple of letters, discard one of them. He also knew that letters and paper could be traced, but that's where dollar stores and Walmart would come in. With each trip to a new area, Sean planned to buy small lots of paper and envelopes, along with self-adhesive stamps. He had learned from of all the CSI and Discovery Channel crime shows that even the water used to wet an envelope could be traced, not to mention the DNA his saliva could provide; therefore, he'd only buy self-adhesive envelopes and stamps.

He also needed to buy latex gloves, along with tweezers, so that any item he touched would be free of fingerprints. Ziploc bags were also on his list. They could be used to transport the letters from the clean room to the mail drop, again so that he wouldn't leave any fingerprints.

As Sean reviewed his list, he thought, *Planning, planning, planning. Don't leave anything to chance.* Throughout the dreary winter months, he compiled his stash of items to be used for the kidnapping and ransom demands. His next step would be more surveillance.

* * *

As winter eased into early spring, Sean was in New England on business. Earlier on his drive north, he had stopped in again at the Watuppa Country Club. His intentions were to just stop by, see what he could see, and continue his drive up to New England. As he pulled into Watuppa's long drive, he noticed the sycamore buds were now showing. It wouldn't be too long until the buds broke and the leaves were out again, offering shade and color to the fading, dim winter landscape. The budding leaves also would offer Sean a good amount of cover within the wood line.

He took the turn to the maintenance road, which led him to the spot where he had parked on previous occasions. It offered him the best view through the trees, bushes, and laurels to the back of the Winslow estate. Besides seeing Watuppa's landscapers, who were busy with their tractors preparing the course for its upcoming season, Sean saw that the Winslows had several workers out and about on their property. In the shrubs, landscapers were raking leaves, while others were busy edging the grass around the flowerbeds that surrounded the large stone patio.

After a minute or two of watching the workers, he noticed a younger lady come into view. She was pushing a stroller with a baby bundled up in it. The stroller was one of those three-wheelers with air tires. Sean thought that was pretty fancy. The woman walked along the outside of the patio area, sort of watching the workers. Then she had a conversation with one of the landscapers as she pointed out things to him.

Wow, Sean thought. *That must be Mrs. Winslow, and that has to be the new baby.* It was just what Sean had hoped he would see. He exited his car and walked into the wood line to stand by some laurel bushes that were quite tall and kept their fat, heavy leaves throughout the winter. With this cover, Sean could spend a little more time observing Mrs. Winslow without anyone noticing him.

For the next five minutes or so, Mrs. Winslow walked around the perimeter of her patio and backyard. A couple of times she went into what looked like a small garden house, as it had part of its roof covered in glass. The baby seemed like he was sleeping as Mrs. Winslow pushed him in his stroller everywhere she went. Sean didn't want to stay too long and decided to leave for now. He'd stop by again on his way back from New England.

The rest of the drive north was exhilarating. He'd had his first glimpse of Mrs. Winslow and the baby. The plan to kidnap the baby, now more than ever, seemed real and possible. Today had been a very good day.

Chapter Fourteen
Observations

That evening, Sean called home. Kathryn answered the phone. "Oh, hi, honey. Glad you called. I've been missing you."

"Just how much have you missed me?"

"Oh, a little bit." Kathryn sighed. "I can't wait until you get home."

"Well, hold on to that thought until I get back."

"Where are you now?"

"Near New London, Connecticut. Hey, tonight I saw a pub with a sign that said HAPPY HOUR, LOBSTER TAIL, AND BEER, so naturally, those being my three favorite things, I went in for dinner."

"Oh, go on." Kathryn laughed. "You're a nut.

* * *

Two days later, Sean was returning to Pennsylvania. As planned, he again drove to the Watuppa Country Club. The weather was simply beautiful, probably the nicest day so far that year. Would Mrs. Winslow be out in the yard again today? Sean hoped so.

He parked his car and walked swiftly to his favorite observation spot. As he headed to the big laurel bush that gave him his best concealment, he noticed what appeared to be a playpen on the lawn up by the Winslows' patio. Sean couldn't make out whether the baby was in there. He waited five or ten minutes, but nothing happened. He decided it was time to leave, as he had an appointment out on I-80 west, in the Pocono Mountains in northeast Pennsylvania.

Chapter Fifteen
The Poconos

Sean recently had made inquiries with several Pocono Mountain real estate agencies for a summer lakefront cottage rental. One of the agencies had called him back and had what Sean was looking for—a secluded, cute, two-bedroom bungalow situated on a four-acre lake. This would be a perfect place where he, Kathryn, and the kids could vacation for the summer. It also would be a perfect place to be vacationing with his wife and *three* small children.

Sean drove west on I-80 from New York, leaving the urban sprawl behind him. In just under two hours, he crossed the Delaware Water Gap into Pennsylvania's Pocono Mountains. He turned north and rode up along the famed Delaware River through the national park. The river was visible from the road and moving quite swiftly from the winter snowmelt and the early spring rains. He crossed his fingers that the cottage he was going to look at was as nice and secluded as the real estate agent had described.

As he turned out of the national park, he headed northwest, through forested, tree-lined roads. Just a few miles up the mountain road, he saw the sign for the cottage: COTTAGE FOR RENT. *This must be it*, he thought, as he turned onto the gravel road that led up the mountainside. The road began to flatten out into what seemed to be an old homestead from years gone by. Now it was a cleared field that led down to a small lake probably fed by mountain springs.

Sean spotted the cottage. *God, this looks perfect*, he thought. It was a one-story, white, Victorian-style cottage with wooden shingles. *Kathryn is going to love this place.* Up ahead, he spotted a car parked in the driveway. As Sean parked his car, the real estate agent came out from the cottage to greet him.

"You must be Sean." The agent extended his hand to shake hands with him. As Sean shook the man's hand, greetings were exchanged. The agent, Chris, asked, "Well, is this secluded enough for you?"

"Yes, very nice. The wife and kids will love this place."

"Come on in," Chris said. "I'll show you the inside." Sean followed him into the cottage. The inside was bright and cheery, with numerous windows letting in plenty of sunlight. "It still smells a bit musty, but if the windows are left open for just a day or two, the stale smell will go away."

"You must have a good nose," Sean said. "I don't smell anything. But if there is a smell, my wife will sure smell it. She's got a nose like a bloodhound."

Chris laughed a bit and led Sean into the family room. The room was very open, with a great view through the sliding glass doors across the small deck to the lake. In the kitchen and dining room, Sean could also see across the family room to the water. Off the family room were the two bedrooms with a good-size full bath between them.

Chris showed Sean the master bedroom. "Here you go," he said. "You can see the lake right from bed, and the master bedroom has a door directly to the bathroom. The other bedroom has to enter the bathroom by the front bathroom door only."

"This is really nice." With Sean's comment, Chris moved into the second bedroom."This is also a fair-size room. How many kids did you say you have?"

Sean paused a moment then replied, "Three. Two girls and a boy."

He took a walk down to the lake as he listened to Chris chat about the area. Chris said the lake held some decent bass, crappie, and catfish. Also, the nearest gas station/convenience store was about eight miles away. "As I told you on the phone, it's a bit off the beaten path."

"That's kind of what we're looking for. Where's the closest town?"

"That would be Milford, fifteen miles to the north and east. There you have your grocery store, hardware store, shops—pretty much all the stuff any old town has. It even has a Walmart."

"Oh, that's great. How about a TV and a phone?"

"There isn't any phone or cable where the cottage is, and I doubt very much if you can get a cell signal here, but if you go up the mountain to the gas station, your cell phone should pick up a signal. There's a pay phone there too. As far as TV goes, I don't think you'd get much of a signal without a dish or something. That's the drawback to being out in the sticks."

Sean laughed. "Yeah, I guess you can't have it all."

Back in the cottage, Sean agreed to the summer rental, signed the con-tract, and gave the agent his deposit check. Handing him a copy of the rental agreement and the keys, Chris said, "The rental doesn't officially start until Memorial Day weekend, but no one will be here before then, so if you want to come up here on a weekend to bring stuff up or just stay, go ahead."

"Thanks, Chris. We'll probably do that."

"Okay. Then I'll have someone come up right away and get the water turned back on."

"Thanks again," Sean said as he shook the agent's hand and turned toward his car.

Before driving off, he pulled out his digital camera from the glove box and took a few photos of the cottage and lake to show Kathryn. *Man,* he thought. *This is perfect, and Kathryn will be so surprised!*

Chapter Sixteen
The Surprise

That evening at the Murphy household, Sean, Kathryn, and the girls were finishing dinner. Sean said, "Kathryn, I have a few photos I downloaded, and I want you to look at them."

Kathryn walked over to the kitchen counter where Sean had the laptop stationed. As Sean scrolled down, the first picture was a photo of the cottage.

"That's a cute little house," Kathryn said. "Why are you showing me this?"

"Hold your horses. I have a few more photos I want you to see before I say anything."

Sean's next photo was of the lake. Kathryn saw a lovely grass field going down a small slope to the lake, which was shrouded by large hardwood trees. The edges of the lake were mostly covered in tall grass and cat o' nine tails.

"Check this out," Sean said.

Kathryn looked at the photo and again appealed for an answer as to why was he showing her these pictures.

Sean said, "Not yet. Check out this next one." The next shot was taken from behind and to the side of the cottage so that it offered a view of both the cottage and the lake. "What do you think?"

Kathryn looked at the photo, then back to Sean. "Let's have it, buster. The suspense is killing me. Did you buy this or something?"

Sean laughed. "Well, *something,* I guess. This is my surprise for you. I rented this Pocono cottage for the summer."

"Oh, my God, Sean. You didn't. Did you really?"

"I sure did. I couldn't resist," he said, smiling.

Sean went on to tell Kathryn all about the cottage, the lake, and how wonderful of a summer they all would have. The plan was for Kathryn and the girls to stay at the cottage. Sean would go to work from the cottage and return there on weekends. He also would be able to take two of his three weeks of vacation there.

Kathryn seemed overwhelmed and excited. "All my life I've wanted to have a summer cottage on a lake. The girls and I are going to love it. Thanks, honey! I love you."

Her only concern was that she had hoped to go to California to visit her mother with the girls this summer. Since both of Sean's parents had passed on years earlier and he was an only child, the girls' only remaining grandparent was Kathryn's mom. Kathryn was also an only child, so without aunts, uncles, or cousins, she really wanted the girls to know their grandmother.

Sean knew what he was about to say would never happen, so he said, "Tell your mom to fly out here and visit you."

"You know she won't do that. Mom would never leave her pets, and she's scared to death of flying."

"Well, maybe next summer I can put something together where we all can visit your mom and maybe even go to Disneyland with the kids."

"Oh, that would be wonderful." Kathryn sighed wistfully.

Sean closed the laptop. *Good,* he thought. *That's now a dead issue.*

* * *

As they were lying in bed that evening, Kathryn said, "I still can't believe you rented that cottage for the whole summer."

Sean replied, "Well, if you want, you can show me your appreciation."

Kathryn scooted over to Sean's side of the bed and gave him a passionate kiss. Then she slowly slid under the covers.

Chapter Seventeen
Another Seed Planted

The next morning, Sean came downstairs to the kitchen to find Kathryn making breakfast for the girls. "Good morning, sleepy head," she said.

"Good morning, honey. Hey, how are my sweetie pies this morning?"

"Good morning, Daddy," both girls shouted at once.

Sean bent over to give each girl a good-morning kiss. "Oh, I didn't tell you about the rest of my business trip. I got so excited about the summer rental."

"Tell me. What happened?"

"While I was up in Massachusetts, I stopped by again to visit Nancy and her baby, Ryan."

"Oh, how is she making out? How's the baby?"

"He's good. He's a cute kid. The father must have been good looking, because Nancy isn't a good-looking broad."

"Broad? Who are you, Frank Sinatra?"

"Oh, you know what I mean. Anyway, she's really trying to get her act together." Sean opened the cabinet, looking for the sugar for his coffee. "She told me she interviewed for a rehab job-training program. Apparently it's not easy to get in. She said the program lasts for three months, and if she completes it, they'll help her land a decent job."

"That would be wonderful. I hope for her sake and the baby's, she gets in."

"Yeah, me too," Sean said. "Cross your fingers that she does."

Chapter Eighteen
Surveillance

It was the latter part of April, and Easter already had come and gone. The forsythias were still in bloom, with their little yellow flowers getting ready to fall and make way for the other flowers of spring to make their debut.

Sean had set up another New York area business trip with full intentions of again stopping by his Watuppa Country Club observation spot. After he completed his business calls, he found his observation spot was almost fully concealed. *Perfect*, thought Sean. *By the time I'm ready to execute my plan, the woods will be dense with all the leafed-out underbrush.*

As he made his way to his spot, he saw where Mrs. Winslow and the landscapers had been busy since the last time he had stopped by. The patio was all cleaned up, and the furnishings had been put back out, including a very large stainless-steel gas grill. *God*, he thought. *That grill is almost as big as the hood of my car.*

The entire lawn and bushes had been raked and swept clean of any remaining leaves. All that seemed lacking were the pretty summer flowers along the scattered flowerbeds just off the patio. Mrs. Winslow, like Kathryn, probably would wait until near the end of May to plant the flowers so as to not put them in harm's way of a late-spring frost. Sean's timeline was drawing close.

Before leaving the cover of his surveillance spot, he pulled out a pair of binoculars. He peered at the house and outbuildings—nothing, no security cameras that he could see. *This is good*, Sean thought. *One less thing to worry about.*

Moving slowly back to his car, he began to envision his "Run for the Roses." He played the scene in his mind as it would unfold. Mrs. Winslow would be outside with the baby and either leave the infant alone for a couple of minutes to go to the garden shed or pop back into the house. This would be all the time he would have. He calculated the timing in his head again. *When I was in high school, I could run the hundred-yard dash in 12.9 seconds*, he thought. *I could probably still manage the seventy to eighty yards in less than twenty seconds. Adding in the time it'll take to scoop up the baby and run back to the car, I should be able to be back with the baby inside of a minute. Even if Mrs. Winslow were to come back just after that, she may not notice that the baby is gone for another minute or so. When she finally realizes the baby is gone, it'll probably still take a moment or two for her to register that the baby is truly gone. She'll probably first yell for the child and frantically look around before coming to grips that there was foul play, then scramble for her cell phone to dial 911. The call will probably take a minute or two, followed by a call to her husband. By that time I'll already be on I-95, making my way into New Jersey over the Tappan Zee Bridge. Even with AMBER Alerts, there shouldn't be a problem.*

With that, Sean decided it was time to head home and perhaps start some springtime jogging to get a bit more in shape.

Chapter Nineteen
Deliberation

When Sean pulled into his driveway, he found Kathryn in the front yard, taking advantage of the lovely day and clearing out her flowerbeds, with the girls looking like they were sort of helping. They looked really cute, Sean thought. Both girls had on blue jeans, hooded sweatshirts, and little garden gloves. Before Sean could get out of his car, they were at the car door, bouncing up and down with excitement.

"Hey, my little cuties! Have you been helping Mommy with her gardening?"

"Yeah," they screamed. Sean didn't even go for his briefcase. He scooped up Lauren and held Nichole's hand as he walked over to the flowerbeds, where Kathryn was standing, waiting for her smooch.

"Hi, honey," Sean said.

Kathryn looped her left arm around the back of Sean's neck and leaned in for a hug and a kiss. "Oh, sorry, hon," she said. "I completely forgot about dinner. I didn't thaw anything out. How about pizza?"

Smiling, he said, "Yeah. I'm in a pizza mood." He put Lauren down but not without first giving her some expected tickles. "Hey, come on. Let Daddy go. I have to order us some pizza."

"Yeah, pizza!" the girls chanted.

"Hang in there, honey. I'll change up real quick and give you a hand," Sean said over the girls' cheers. As he turned to walk to the house, he glanced back at Kathryn and said, "You look good covered in dirt."

"Soooo, you like the dirty look?"

"Sure do, you dirty girl."

Kathryn chuckled as Sean entered the house.

Later in the evening, Sean put on his sneakers and headed for the door. Kathryn said, "Where are you going?"

"It's still nice out. I'm going for a quick run to try to work off some of tonight's pizza and a winter's worth of lazy fat."

As Sean jogged through the neighborhood, he thought, *Not bad. I'm not as winded as I thought I'd be. If I keep this up, there should be no problem.* He was right. He was still in pretty good shape. He had a few extra beer and fast-food pounds around the waist but still had a decent physique.

The next morning, Sean was solemn. He'd had a very restless night's sleep. Reality was setting in again. For the millionth time, he questioned himself, wondering whether his plan would work and if it was worth the risk. All night he had tossed and turned, his brain working on overdrive. *Well, today will be decision time*, he thought. *I'll review all the details again and make my decision as to whether to go forward or call it quits.*

When Sean went downstairs, Kathryn was getting ready to take the children out with her on some errands. She turned to him and said, "Good morning, hon. Are you sure you don't have time to watch the girls this morning?"

"I only wish. I'll be buried most of the day with reports. When you get home, could you try to keep the girls down to a mild roar?"

Kathryn told him she'd probably be home by noon and that the girls would more than likely take a nap right after lunch. "Not to worry. You'll have plenty of quiet time to do your work," she said.

"Thanks. Have a good time."

After Kathryn and the girls left, Sean retreated to his basement room to once again review every detail of his plan. He went over everything he had done and prepared for to date. He was pleased with how well things had gone so far. Next would be the actual kidnapping itself and bringing home the baby boy. He wasn't so nervous about bringing the baby home; he felt his plan for that would work flawlessly. He was very nervous, however, about taking the baby. If the kidnapping scenario turned out to be a good one, he would go for it. If it wasn't the perfect scenario, then so be it, no deal. In Sean's mind, fate would decide whether the kidnapping would take place.

Chapter Twenty
Collecting the Ransom

Sean had reviewed his plan for collecting the ransom as much as he had worked through all the other details. The Winslows were very wealthy, and between Jim's parents and grandparents, there should be no problem raising the $1.3 million in unmarked used cash that he would ask for, especially with the timeframe he had in mind. The reason for the odd sum of money was to confuse the FBI as to why he was requesting that particular amount. Was it money lost in the stock market—someone's retirement perhaps? It would at least throw a small curve into the FBI's creating a profile of who would do such a thing.

Immediately after the kidnapping took place, Sean would drop a pre-written letter into a local mailbox on his way to the highway. The letter would let the Winslows know that their baby was doing fine and that under no circumstances would any harm come to the child. Sean would make this very clear. The letter also would mention that all correspondence would come only by US mail.

Sean's plan was still to regularly assure the Winslows that their baby was doing fine. He wouldn't mention the ransom until about the fourth letter. Sean figured by then they would at least feel that the baby was okay and would be a bit calmer.

For the ransom collection to work, Sean felt he had to keep up his one-way communication, constantly assuring the parents that their child was well and including photos of the baby. He also knew that because the Winslows were very wealthy and had powerful connections, this crime would be investigated to the hilt. He was sure the FBI and hired private investigators would turn over every rock possible. They would investigate disgruntled employees of the firm, clients who had lost large amounts of money investing with Winslow and McClure, all friends of the Winslows, and household employees—basically anyone who had contact with the family.

The FBI, however, wouldn't have much to go on, as they'd only have Sean's letters to analyze, forensically and profile-wise, along with anything from the crime scene. Sean felt that after a couple of months the Winslows would lose faith in the FBI's abilities to bring their child home and would begin to feel the best way to get their child back would be to go along with the demands of the kidnapper.

By the time Sean had reviewed all of his concerns and the details of his plan, Kathryn was back home with the girls and lunch was ready. So was his kidnapping plan.

Chapter Twenty-One
The Cottage

That weekend, Sean and Kathryn prepared for their trip to the cottage in the Poconos. Sean packed the garage with all the essentials they'd need to start their summer vacation by the lake. Since the realtor had said they could move in early, Sean thought it would be good to get Kathryn and the girls moved from their home in Pennsylvania and located in the remote mountain house.

"Hey, hon," he said, "since the realtor said we could get into the cottage early, why don't we go up next Friday, the week before Memorial Day weekend? That way I can leave right from the Poconos to New England, saving some time in my travel, and the same when I return. It'll also give me a little extra time with you and the girls before summer starts."

Kathryn's only concern, she said, was whether it would still be cool up in the mountains. He replied, "Probably just early in the morning and toward evening, but we'll have a fireplace. I'll make sure to have everything ready before I go on my trip."

"Good. I don't want us girls to freeze."

"Oh, it won't be that cold. It'll just be cool."

* * *

The following weekend, Sean and Kathryn drove separately up to the summer cottage. From their house, the travel time to the cottage was a bit less than two hours, and that included two bathroom stops. *Girls*, thought Sean.

When they arrived, Kathryn couldn't believe how beautiful it was. With the spring leaves, the area was even prettier than the photos Sean had shown Kathryn. The girls seemed to be equally excited, running, playing, and yelling. Kathryn hugged Sean and said, "Thank you for this. It'll be a wonderful summer." With that they embraced and kissed for a long time.

"Come on, Kathryn. I'll show you the house."

"Come on, girls!" she yelled. "Let's go see the house and your new bedroom."

With the girls in tow, Sean showed the family their summer retreat. Everything was perfect. Sean also had arranged with the realtor to have the house cleaned so that it would be extra nice and smell fresh when Kathryn and the girls arrived.

Kathryn loved the cottage layout. "It's so cute and lovely," she said.

"I knew you'd love it. I'll go get the stuff from the car. You can start fixing things up."

That weekend was wonderful, with the weather cooperating—low fifties in the evenings and early mornings, with a high in the seventies during the day and plenty of sunshine. The evening fires were warm and very romantic.

When Monday morning came, Sean got up early, not waking anyone, and added a couple of logs to the hot embers in the fireplace. He headed out on his trip, but instead of going straight to New England, he drove back home to Pennsylvania to pick up his supplies, in case "things" worked out.

Chapter Twenty-Two
The Shakes

Back at their house in Pennsylvania, Sean checked the Internet for an extended weather forecast for Rye, New York, where the Winslows lived. The forecast called for more of the same good weather with a warming trend for at least the next five days. *This is good*, Sean thought. *Very good. Mrs. Winslow will more than likely be spending time in her yard.*

He reviewed his list of things to bring. First was the baby harness he'd use to carry the child while he ran back to his vehicle. Baby clothes, a blanket, a baby car seat, stroller, diapers, wipes, a juice bottle—he had all the things a mother would send with her child. Sean also packed up his first prewritten letter in a plastic bag, free of any forensic evidence. He also had some stolen Rhode Island license plates, which he had removed from a car in a dimly lit parking lot on his last trip to Rhode Island. He would magnetically fasten the Rhode Island plates over his Pennsylvania plates just before entering the grounds of the Watuppa Country Club.

After Sean organized his gear and loaded it into the car, he headed north up to New York to the country club. It was about noon now, and it would be close to two p.m. by the time he arrived.

Sean felt a new feeling each time he went to Watuppa. His first trip was one of awe. On later trips he felt excitement, and now he felt a surge of adrenaline mixed with nervousness. *Oh, God*, he thought. *Am I actually going to do this?* He pulled over to where he usually parked and made a bigger loop on the drive to see if the maintenance crew was around. The coast was clear. He parked his car horizontally this time, so that the passenger-side back door was more accessible. He grabbed the baby harness off the seat and quickly made his way into the wooded timberline.

As Sean approached his concealed staging area, he heard the sounds of lawnmowers. When he looked up at the Winslow house, he saw landscapers hard at work, taking care of the grounds.

As quickly as Sean surveyed the situation, he was out of there, walking briskly back to his vehicle. Back inside his car, he was breathing heavily and feeling a bit faint. *Oh, wow*, he thought. *I'm actually shaking.* He waited a few moments to settle down then drove calmly down the long country club drive. Within a few minutes, he was on I-95, headed north to handle a business call as though nothing had happened. Sean's travels that day took him a bit north, around the Bridgeport, Connecticut area, where he settled in for the evening at a hotel. Room service and a movie would fit the bill for the night, and hopefully he'd get a decent night's sleep.

Chapter Twenty-Three
Run for the Roses

On Tuesday, May 23, Sean awoke to the alarm in his hotel room. He was shocked to have slept the whole night through, as he rarely got a good night's sleep while on the road, especially with everything that had buzzed around in his mind these last few days. As if it were a typical day, he cleaned up, got dressed, and headed to the hotel restaurant for breakfast. Afterward he checked his messages, made a couple of business phone calls, and proceeded again to drive south to New York to scope out the Winslows' home.

When he arrived at Watuppa, he drove through the club's main gate. Unlike yesterday, he was much more observant to the spring-like conditions of the entranceway and course. Many of the early spring flowers were in bloom, and he saw some dogwoods with little white blooms at the ends of theirs branches and yellow day lilies scattered here and there. The entranceway itself was landscaped with tulips, irises, and daffodils, and the trees along the driveway had leaves budding out.

This place is truly beautiful, Sean thought. *Perhaps someday I too will be a member of a private golf club.* He briefly fantasized about what it would be like to be greeted by name when he walked into the club and what it would be like to enter the men's locker room and see his name inscribed on an ornate brass plate above his locker. He thought about how, after a great round of golf on a beautifully groomed course, he could have a wonderful lunch and drinks in the grillroom, followed by a nice shower, a steam, then a cooling rinse-off shower, and when he got back to his locker to change up, his shoes would be polished. This was first class, and perhaps this caper would provide him the means to realize such a dream.

Like the day before, Sean circled his car around, checking to see whether anyone was about. It was just after ten a.m., so no golfers would have made their way around yet to the seventeenth hole, and he didn't see any maintenance workers. He parked horizontally again, grabbed the baby harness and his leather gloves, and moved into the thick laurel bushes. Yesterday he had heard the noise of the lawn mowers, but today he heard the fussing sounds of a baby. He looked up at the Winslows' house and saw the baby standing, holding onto the playpen's top railing, crying out for something. It wasn't a cry of pain; it was just a fussing cry. After a moment he saw woman, most likely Mrs. Winslow, come over to the playpen and grab what looked like a juice bottle from a large bag and give it to the baby. Instantly the child grabbed the bottle, and with his little hands, he held it in the air and up to his mouth. Then he plopped down on his bottom and continued to drink. The woman stood there a moment and watched the baby drinking his bottle. Then she walked over by a row of small bushes, where she knelt to plant some flowers she had in a little garden wagon.

It seemed like an eternity for Sean, but in reality it was only about a half-an-hour since he had started to observe the woman and the baby. By that time it appeared that the baby had fallen asleep, and the woman was moving along, continuing to plant her colorful flowers. As Sean watched, the woman got up from her knees, stretched a bit, and walked over to where the baby lay in the playpen. She leaned in and adjusted the baby's blanket.

After covering him, she walked over to her garden cart and picked up an empty black tray that probably had held all the flowers. She held it over the area of her newly planted flowers, then tapped the back of it to remove any remaining potting soil inside. Then she dropped the carton back in the wagon, grabbed the wagon by its handle, spun it around, and headed toward the garden shed. Sean's heart pounded and raced as the adrenaline kicked in. He knew this might be his opportunity to snatch the baby.

The woman pulled the cart over to the garden shed and rounded the corner, vanishing from sight. That very moment, Sean sprang from his hiding spot in the woods and began his seventy-yard sprint across the cut grass toward the playpen. In less than twenty seconds, he was breathing very heavily next to the playpen, looking down at the baby, who was sleeping. He took one quick look toward the garden shed and saw no sign of anyone. Without hesitation, he leaned in, gently scooped up the baby, and in one fell swoop, had the baby out of the crib and up against his chest and was sliding him into the harness. He turned and ran back to the wood line.

As he ran, he used his arms and hands to cradle and support the baby, but to his surprise, the baby didn't fuss or cry. As Sean neared the woods, he glanced over his shoulder and still didn't see the woman. *Great*, he thought. *Just a little bit more to go. Baby, don't cry. We're almost there.*

He was now entering the wood line and the secure cover of the laurel bushes. As he moved to the outer inside edge, he once again peeked back to the Winslow house—good, still no one around. He quickly surveyed the area for maintenance workers or any witnesses who might see him with the baby, but no one was around. Sean's mind raced along with his breathing. *Just another ten yards to the rear passenger door*, he thought. By now the baby was fussing a bit but wasn't making any loud cries. He was just letting Sean know that he was either uncomfortable or wanted to do something else. Either way the car door was open. Sean took the baby from his chest pouch and plopped him into the car seat.

Before reaching for the baby-seat straps, Sean grabbed a big sugar cookie from a bag on the seat. The baby seemed to recognize it immediately, because once he got hold of it, the cookie went directly into his mouth. *Oh, man,* Sean thought. *How good is this?* The baby was quiet now and secure in the car seat. Sean climbed into the driver's seat. As he was closing the door, he paused for a moment to listen. *Good*, he thought. *I haven't heard anyone scream out or cry. Mrs. Winslow is still probably unaware that her child is gone.* The car was now in drive and headed out of the grounds of Watuppa Country Club.

Chapter Twenty-Four
The Getaway

Sean knew this route by heart, and everything within him wanted to drive faster, but he retained his composure and stayed at a safe and normal speed. As he motored up the street, he pulled over to a USPS mailbox. He opened the Ziploc bag, and with his thin leather gloves on, dropped the envelope into the mailbox. He wanted the note to get to the Winslows as soon as possible.

Moments later he was on I-95 south, on his way to his home in Pennsylvania, where he would spend the night and much of the next day hidden away. After driving south over the George Washington Bridge, he entered the New Jersey Turnpike. A few minutes later, the traffic started to jam up and slow down. *Oh, no,* he thought. He remembered that an easy way to capture criminals driving on highways was for the state police to go ahead of where they suspected the criminal to be and to slow down traffic. This would give the police a chance to drive up the freeway in the breakdown lane, checking cars as they drove past.

Sean's stomach churned as the traffic slowed to a near stop. Quickly he switched on the AM radio to the news station to hear whether there was any information about why the traffic had slowed down. "Commercials. Shit," Sean muttered as he switched to another station, where the chopper-in-the-sky reporter announced that a three-car accident had been reported on the southbound side of the New Jersey turnpike. Traffic was at a crawl from exit thirteen to exit twelve. That seemed to calm Sean down, but until he passed the accident scene, he had the jitters.

He finally arrived in Pennsylvania and pulled into his neighborhood of typical suburban tract homes. As he drove down his street, he looked around to see whether anyone was out and about. No one. *Good*, thought Sean. *Probably because everyone is still at work and the children are in school.* He hit the garage door opener and drove into the garage, with the door closing behind him.

"Well, little feller," Sean said to the baby, as he took him from the backseat, "it looks like it's you and me baching it for a couple of days."

Chapter Twenty-Five
Where's My Ryan?

Back at the Winslow residence, the nightmare had begun. Molly Winslow had returned from the garden shed with her wagon full of tiny pink geraniums. She pulled the wagon up to where she had left off planting. Before kneeling down to plant again, she walked over to check on the baby. It took her a moment to realize the baby wasn't in the playpen. Then it took another moment for her mind to register what her eyes were telling her. Her baby wasn't there. *Dear God*, she thought. *My baby is gone!*

Just as Sean had expected, Molly cried out for the baby, "Ryan, Ryan. Where are you? Ryan, Ryan! Ryan, where are you?" Molly shrieked out Ryan's name while quickly and frantically looking in and around the bushes. Where the hell had her baby gone? Could he have crawled out of the playpen? How? Could someone have taken her baby? Who? Why? Who could do this to her? Molly's mind swirled with confusion and fear. Could her husband have come home early? Was he inside the house with the baby? She ran for the kitchen door off the back patio. As she pulled the door open, she yelled, "Jim!" No reply came. "Oh, God!" Molly screamed hysterically as she picked up the phone and frantically dialed 911.

Chapter Twenty-Six
Safe at Home

Back home in Pennsylvania, Sean had the baby on a table in his basement clean room. He put a white sheet up to use as a backdrop. Leaning against the sheet was a copy of that day's *USA Today* that he had taken from his hotel room that morning.

The old Polaroid Instamatic flashed, and Sean had a picture of the baby with the newspaper in the background. Still wearing gloves, he used a pair of tweezers to pull the photo from the camera and then placed it down to develop. He went over to the baby, picked him up, and put him on the rug to play.

Again, no problems from the baby. *God*, Sean thought. *He's such a good kid. I wish mine were as easy to handle when they were his age.* He went back to the photo, using the tweezers to peel back the cover, which revealed a nice shot of the baby with the newspaper next to him. He placed the photo in an envelope, used the tweezers to peel off a self-adhesive stamp, and then affixed it to the envelope. Next he sealed the self-adhesive envelope he had pread-dressed to the Winslows. With that complete he placed the envelope inside a Ziploc bag to be mailed in the New York area on Thursday. Afterward, Sean fed the baby and then covered his ass with sales calls made from home.

Chapter Twenty-Seven
The Nightmare Begins

That day at the Winslow home, things couldn't have been any worse. The Winslows' baby had been taken. Jim Winslow was Molly's second call after the 911 call. It was hard for Jim to understand what the heck she was saying, as she was completely hysterical. Her crying had turned into heavy sobbing, and her words came out slurred. At that point, without hearing all the details clearly, Jim knew something was very wrong and that it involved Ryan.

Without waiting for Molly to calm down or collect herself, Jim moved rapidly out of his office. As he passed his secretary's desk, he told her to send the police immediately to his house, as something had gone wrong, and that he was on his way home.

Jim's secretary heard the urgency in his voice and didn't say a word as Jim was already moving past her and out of the office. She did as told and called information for the Rye, New York, police and relayed Jim's request to have officers go to his house. She had no other information to give the police, other than she was sure this was definitely serious.

By the time Jim had gotten to his car in the office building's garage, Molly had composed herself enough to relate to him that someone must have snatched their baby while she was planting flowers by the back patio.

As Jim continued to try to calm Molly down, the police, who had responded to the 911 call, had arrived. Through the phone, Jim heard Molly, hysterical again, trying to tell the officers what had happened. Jim drove as

Ransom By Mail

rapidly through the Manhattan traffic as he could, and one of the officers had taken the phone from Molly and spoke directly to Jim. The officer reviewed what Molly had said and told Jim they had summoned the paramedics just in case Molly needed them. Jim told the officers that he was on his way and would call the family doctor. He said he also would call his family from his car. The officer told Jim to go ahead and make his calls and assured him that if anything more came up that he would immediately call Jim back.

After nearly an hour of frantic driving through the notorious Manhattan traffic and up the throughway, Jim finally arrived home. On the way, besides talking again to Molly, Jim had spoken to his father, the family doctor, and again to the local cops at the house. By the time Jim arrived, Molly had been given a sedative by their doctor, who had shot right over to the house once Jim had told him what had happened. Jim's parents and in-laws were also coming over. No one could make any sense of it, except to say that more than likely it was a kidnap for ransom. That would certainly be the lesser of the two evils, and with the Winslows being a wealthy family, it made sense to assume there had been a kidnapping for money.

At least the sedative the doctor had given Molly would help her get some sleep. The rest of the Winslow family wouldn't have it so easy.

The rest of the day was filled with talking to the authorities and discussing possible scenarios of what might have happened. Who could do such a thing? Would the baby be okay? Would the kidnapper call right away? Many of these unanswered questions tortured their minds throughout the day and long into the night.

66

Chapter Twenty-Eight
First Letter

Wednesday morning, the day after the kidnapping, and still no ransom call. Molly had awoken. Although she felt a bit better, she was still a bundle of nerves. While Jim's father and Molly's dad were busy downstairs in the den with the police and now the FBI, Molly's mother-in-law and mother were in Molly and Jim's bedroom, trying in vain to calm Molly down and offer some comfort.

The FBI was retrieving all the information from the Winslows they could get, such as the names of household and Watuppa Country Club employees, friends, possible business or personal enemies, contractors, and disgruntled customers from the brokerage firm, Winslow and McClure. The questions kept coming, and the Winslows provided all they could to help the FBI. Still, a single question haunted them: "Who could do such a horrid thing to us?"

Later that morning, the mail arrived. In the mail was the prewritten letter Sean had dropped into the mailbox moments after the kidnapping. The letter was addressed to Mr. and Mrs. Winslow with a return address of "Baby Winslow, 1 Lula Bye Rd., New York, NY."

When Jim saw this, he immediately knew what this was and discarded the other mail on the nearest table. Without alerting anyone, he moved into his study, where he was alone, and carefully opened the letter. His hands slightly shaking, he held the letter up to the morning light that came in from the large multi-paned window in his study and began to read.

Mr. and Mrs. Winslow:

This letter is to inform you that I am the person who kidnapped your baby. Your son is perfectly fine and is in no danger whatsoever. Also, I have no intention of causing him any harm. This is a kidnap for ransom, and if this kidnap for ransom is unsuccessful or terminated, I will not harm your son. Your only concern will be whether you get to see your son again, and that is entirely up to you.

I assume you have contacted all the authorities, and everything will be monitored. I will save you some additional anguish in waiting for a ransom call, as there will be NO PHONE CALLS. All correspondence will be sent to you through the US mail. I know this is a slower process, but again, the baby is fine, and he's living in a good, nurturing environment.

You will receive regular updates regarding your child. The next letter has been mailed and should arrive by Friday.

Jim reread the letter a few times to make sure he didn't miss anything. His biggest fear for the moment, the baby's safety, was answered. He went to the copy machine in his office and made himself a copy before calling over the authorities to review the letter. He gave them the letter with the envelope and then summoned Molly and his parents into the study. As the Winslows and Molly's parents, the Sullivans, entered the study, Jim announced that he had received the first correspondence from the kidnapper.

Everyone held his or her breath as Jim read the letter aloud. After the letter was read, Molly reached over to Jim's hand, wanting to read it herself. She would read that letter over and over throughout that day. After Molly read the letter again, the copy was passed around, with everyone trying to be supportive, saying, "Well, the kidnapper does make it very clear that the baby is okay and that no harm will come to him. For now that's the most important thing."

Chapter Twenty-Nine
Cousin Ryan

On Wednesday evening, Sean was in the garage of his house, packing his vehicle with all of the baby's stuff. He wanted to wait until the neighborhood was settled in for the night. Then, under the cover of darkness, he'd drive out of the neighborhood and north up to the Poconos vacation home with the baby.

Later that night, as Sean pulled up to the summer cottage, Ryan was sound asleep in his baby seat. For the first part of the drive up to the Poconos, the baby fussed a little, but Sean went for his ace in the hole, the sugar cookie. After the cookie and some juice, the baby drifted off. Sean saw the lights on in the vacation home, so he knew Kathryn was still up. He opened and closed his car door quietly, so as not to wake the baby, and walked to the little cottage, then tapped on the glass of the locked front door.

Kathryn almost jumped out of her flannel pajamas, which had a little teddy bear pattern on them. Sean said quietly through the door, "Hi, hon. It's me."

She got up and opened the door. "You scared me half to death! I didn't expect you until the end of the week." Sean leaned in and gave her a big kiss.

As he dragged his luggage through the door, he said, "I had something come up and needed to get back early." He let go of the bag and grabbed Kathryn by the hand. "Are the kids asleep?"

"Yes," she said. "They played by the lake all day. They were pooped."

"Good. That's good. I need to talk to you for a moment."

"What is it?" asked Kathryn, eyeing Sean curiously. "Is everything okay? Did something happen at work?"

"Yes, everything's all right, but I have a big favor to ask of you."

"Okay, what?"

"Well, when I arrived in Massachusetts, I stopped in again to see Nancy and her baby, Ryan."

"How's she doing?"

"Just fine. She's come a long way, and she's waiting to enter the rehab job-training program. It's a chance for her to clean up and acquire good job skills."

"That would be wonderful."

"Well," Sean, taking a deep breath, said, "the problem is that she can't go to the rehab training center with her baby. Her choice is to have her loony mom look after her child while she goes away for the three months, or the state could put the child into a temporary foster home. Nancy said that neither would work for her, so she was going to have to pass on the opportunity for the time being."

"That's awful," Kathryn said with a sigh.

"Yeah," said Sean. "This is where that favor I mentioned comes in."

"Oh, God, Sean. What did you volunteer me for?"

Sean stood up. "Hold on a moment. I've got something for you in the car." He quickly walked out of the cottage and retrieved little Ryan. As he walked back to the front door, Kathryn stood there waiting. She looked at the little bundle Sean was carrying, and from the way he was carrying it, she knew instantly what the surprise was. Sean spoke very softly and said, "Honey, meet little Ryan."

"Oh, my God, Sean. He's so precious!"

Sean said, "Honey, I'm sorry. I just had to do this for Nancy. I truly felt it was the right thing to do."

As Sean handed the baby to Kathryn, he said, "Well, can we take care of him until Nancy completes her job training?"

"Oh, you big, soft slob," Kathryn said. "Of course. You *are* a big, soft slob, you know. But that's one of the reasons I married you."

Sean leaned in across the sleeping baby and gave Kathryn a big kiss. "Thanks, honey. You're the best. I'll go get his stuff from the car. I've got a letter from Nancy for you."

When Sean returned from the car with loads of baby gear, Kathryn already had a blanket on the floor near the fireplace with the baby sleeping on it and another blanket covering him up. "Beautiful, isn't he?" said Kathryn. "Just wait until the girls see him."

"Yeah," Sean said, putting down the baby gear. "He'll be a living doll for them to play with."

Sean handed a letter to Kathryn, supposedly from Nancy. When Sean wrote the letter, he used his best cursive handwriting, taught to him by who he would call the Sisters of No Mercy at St. Joseph's Elementary School. The nuns had taught him well. Sean used to joke that he had the scars on his knuckles to prove it. The letter read:

> Dear Kathryn,
>
> Thank you so much for caring for Ryan while I get my life back in order. Sean has always been there for me, and I want to thank you too for this. I know you will give Ryan lots of love and attention, and I promise to someday be able to repay you for your kindness.
>
> I have a lot to do in the months ahead, and I have promised myself to do my very best. Thanks for helping me with this opportunity.
>
> Love,
>
> Nancy

Kathryn said, "I do hope the very best for her. It's a very nice note. Here, Sean. Read it." As she handed Sean the letter, she said, "Oh, my. Nancy sure packed up a ton of food and stuff for the baby. Good. That'll save me from having to run into town tomorrow."

"Speaking of things you may need," Sean said, "I have to head up to Connecticut tomorrow to finish my sales calls, but I'll be back before evening. Make a list of anything you think you'll need, and I'll pick it up on my way home."

The next morning, the entire Murphy household was up with the cry of a little baby. The girls heard it too and came running into Sean and Kathryn's bedroom.

"Mommy, Daddy, who's the little baby?" asked Nichole.

Kathryn said, "That's your baby cousin, Ryan. He's going to stay with us for a while. Isn't he a little cutie?" The girls hovered over the baby, touching and kissing his soft, chubby cheeks.

Sean smiled. "I see you have two little babysitter assistants to help you out."

"Yeah," Kathryn said. "Including you, I now have four children to take care of."

Chapter Thirty
Looking Good

As Sean drove east on I-80 from the Poconos into New York, he passed over the George Washington Bridge. Shortly thereafter he took an exit and looked for a mailbox. He wanted to make sure the letter had a New York postmark. He took out the Ziploc bag with the letter inside, pulled out his tweezers, and carefully dropped the letter into the mailbox.

Soon after, Sean was on I-95, headed into Connecticut. As he drove north, he passed the Rye exit to the Watuppa Country Club. *Man, I did it,* thought Sean. *Now all I have to do is be very careful, stay smart, and stick to the plan.* During the drive into Connecticut, his mind was filled with a review of the next steps he would take. From this point on, patience would be a key factor. For the ransom plan to work, Sean would have to gain the trust of Molly Winslow.

He figured that if no one had seen him or his car at the Watuppa Country Club on the day of the kidnapping, the FBI wouldn't have much to go on. If the only correspondence was from sterile letters mailed in the New York metro area, it would limit the scope of their investigation.

Sean was sure the FBI would analyze the letters for content to try to create a profile for the kidnapper or kidnappers, but this wouldn't yield them much. His writing and grammar would probably indicate that the kidnapper had some college education or was a college graduate. That was okay with

Sean, as he felt it better if the Winslows knew they were dealing with someone with some intelligence. This would play into his favor.

Sean also figured that the profile might be many things, but certainly not a young, happily married man with two children, a home, and a decent job. This scenario would go against all normal thinking and behavior. So Sean's thoughts went again to why the hell he would do such a thing. Probably the same reason he had blown last year's $4,000 bonus from ZAP betting on the underdog Philadelphia Eagles over the New York Giants in the division play-off and never mentioning the bonus or the loss to Kathryn. Or why he'd had sex in his neighbor's basement with his neighbor's wife while a neighborhood party was going on upstairs. However, this was different. This was high stakes, all in, the ultimate bet. His whole life—and the lives of his family—was riding on it. Although the odds were against him, and as crazy as this might be, Sean felt confident in his plan.

Chapter Thirty-One
Second Letter

Before the mail was even delivered to the Winslows' home on Friday morning, the FBI was at the local post office intercepting the second letter. After the letter was quickly processed, the Winslows received a copy of it, along with a copy of the accompanying photo.

> Mr. and Mrs. Winslow:
>
> As you can see from the enclosed photo, your boy is doing well. He is a very happy baby and already has adjusted well to his new environment.
>
> Updates will continue with eventual instructions for the ransom and the return of your child.
>
> Again, do not worry about the well-being of your baby. He is fine.

Jim and Molly were the only ones home, except for a couple of FBI agents. Molly broke down again after seeing the picture of Ryan. Wrapped up in her husband's arms, she cried about how badly she wanted her baby back. Jim's only comfort to her was that all seemed well with the baby and that the kidnapper had assured them again that the child was fine. The two agents quietly moved to the next room to leave Jim and Molly alone.

Chapter Thirty-Two
Walmart

As soon as Sean finished his lunch date at a medical center in upstate New York, he headed to the summer cottage for the weekend. When he arrived, everyone was in the living room, and the girls were on the floor, playing with the baby.

Kathryn said, "Daddy's home!" The girls left the baby and rushed to their father's arms.

"Hey!" Smiling at the girls, Sean asked, "Have you been helping Mommy with the baby?" Yeses were in the air from both of them. Tickles ensued, with Nichole taking her daddy by the hand over to the baby on the floor and showing him how she gave him big hugs.

"You were right," Kathryn said. "He's their living baby doll. They haven't left his side all day."

Sean got up. "That's great. How's the little guy doing?"

"Oh, just fine. He's a really good boy."

Kathryn and Sean went to the kitchen to finish preparing dinner. Kathryn took the pot of macaroni and cheese off the stove and stirred it. "I took the girls and the baby into town to pick up some supplies today."

Sean's heart fell to his stomach. Holding back his nervousness, he said calmly, "Where did you go?"

"Where else? Walmart, my favorite store."

"You drove all the way to Milford?"

79

"Yes, it's really not that long of a drive, and it's a pretty one. You should have seen the looks I got with the three little ones. One lady said, 'Boy, you've got your hands full.' "

Thoughts flew through Sean's head. Shit! What if Kathryn bought a newspaper or heard something on TV as she strolled past the electronics department? He bit his lip and took a deep breath as he fiddled with the silverware and set the table. He calmly said, "So what did you say to her?"

"I told her the two girls are mine and that the little boy is their cousin."

Sean paused a moment. "Good answer. I wouldn't want people thinking I was a sex maniac."

"Yeah, if they only knew!"

Later that evening, while they were getting ready for bed, Sean said, "Hey, hon, if anyone else asks you about Ryan, please don't say he's our cousin's child. That'll lead to an explanation, and I don't want to discuss Nancy's problems with anyone. I'd like to keep that private."

Kathryn looked puzzled. "What do you want me to say?"

"Just play along that the child is ours. It'll end in a compliment, and they'll think your husband is a sex maniac."

"Or that *I* am."

Both of them laughed as they got into bed. *God,* Sean thought. *I'll have to be better about keeping Kathryn at the cottage and away from the public.*

Chapter Thirty-Three
FBI

Letters three and four arrived Wednesday of that week and the following Wednesday. Each letter closely repeated the mantra of what the second letter had said, with the fourth letter containing an additional photo of Ryan with another recent *USA Today* newspaper next to him. Sean was sure this would give some comfort to the Winslows and that they might feel a bit more secure about their baby being safe. This eventually would lend itself to Sean's plan of Mrs. Winslow trusting him to return their child.

Again, Sean had mailed each letter from the New York metro area, as he was hoping to keep the FBI focused on New York. After the fourth letter had arrived, the entire Winslow clan, including Jim's father, had a sit-down progress report with the FBI. Special Agent Lacher reviewed the facts of the case thus far. He started by saying he was sorry about this awful situation and that he and the FBI were using all their resources to apprehend the kidnapper and safely return the baby to the Winslows.

"With that said," Agent Lacher continued, "let me bring you up to speed with what we have so far. We know the baby was kidnapped from the rear of the house next to the seventeenth hole of country club. The FBI located the probable staging area from which the house was more than likely staked out and from where the actual kidnapping took place. Unfortunately no physical evidence was found, as the ground was fairly dry, and no shoe or tire impressions were good enough for us to use. Also, no other forensic signs were left at either the playpen or by the kidnapper's stakeout area."

He went on to say that the FBI had interviewed all the Watuppa Country Club groundskeepers, other employees, and outside contractors. None of them seemed to be connected in any way to the kidnapping. Also, none of them had noticed any person or vehicle in or around the stakeout area the morning of the kidnapping or any time earlier. The letters received thus far hadn't revealed anything in the way of forensic trace evidence. The paper, envelopes, and stamps were all standard and could be purchased at any OfficeMax, dollar store, or Walmart. The postmarks on the letters and the kidnapper's knowledge of the area led the FBI to believe that he was living in or around the New York area.

The FBI was investigating the list of past and present employees of Winslow and McClure that the family had provided. So far none of them seemed to be connected to the crime. The FBI also reviewed videotapes of cars entering all the local toll areas, bridges, tunnels, and highways to see whether a baby could be seen in anyone's vehicle. If they did see a baby in someone's car, they'd run the plate and investigate, but nothing to date had provided any leads.

As far as profiling the kidnapper went, the FBI believed him to be a male in his late twenties to mid-thirties, favoring the mid-thirties, and in fairly decent shape, as they presumed he would have had to run from the stakeout area to the house and back. Also, by the content of the kidnappers letters, they felt he had attended college for a few years or had graduated college. He might have a criminal background, but he was definitely used to taking risks. Possibly he liked bungee jumping or that sort of thing, because he apparently enjoyed risks and danger; the FBI told the Winslows that those go hand-in-hand. They said he might also be a gambler, but that was a maybe, as he hadn't yet asked for the ransom. If he were a dedicated gambler, he would have wanted the money as soon as he could get it.

The FBI also felt the kidnapper probably had an accomplice who helped him take care of the baby. It could be a wife, girlfriend, or a hired nanny. Many of the nannies in New York City, they said, are illegal and not traceable. Also, many of the nannies in Manhattan don't speak English and therefore probably wouldn't know they were watching a kidnapped child.

In New York City, they said, it wouldn't be suspicious to see a couple walking with a young child. Hell, today not many people even know their neighbors.

After Molly heard everything the FBI agents had to say, she spoke up, interrupting the agent. "Excuse me, Agent Lacher. So if I get what you're telling us, you don't have anything to go on. Am I right?"

Agent Lacher replied, "Not exactly. We don't have anything at the moment to lead us directly to the kidnapper, but we have been able to eliminate a lot of potentials. This narrows the field of play, and eventually the kidnapper will give us something more to go on. When that happens, the work we're doing now puts us one step closer to apprehending him or them and getting your child back." Agent Lacher began to put all of his papers into a folder and straighten them. "Folks, the FBI has worked many kidnapping cases where it's seemed they were at a dead end, but it just takes one small mistake, one slipup on the part of the kidnapper, and we have him. Please, Mr. and Mrs. Winslow, trust that we know what we're doing and know how to handle this."

Jim's dad, Martin, finally spoke up. "Agent Lacher, what do you want us to do?"

"For the time being, go about your normal lives as much as you can. I certainly know that may seem impossible, but we need you folks to be calm and not stressed so that when the time comes, you'll be in much better mental and physical shape to assist us." Agent Lacher stood up. "I'll be at the house for the rest of the day if any of you wish to talk further."

"Thank you," Jim said." We know you're doing your very best."

Like hell, Molly thought. *I'm not an FBI agent, and I know as much as you do.* But for now she held her tongue.

Chapter Thirty-Four
Cottage Life

The first two weeks of June featured an array of weather changes that caused frequent nighttime thunderstorms. Sean would get the girls together, sit by the big glass door, and watch the lightning strikes in the sky. After each strike, he'd say, "Okay, girls. Let's count. One, two, three, four, barroom." Then the thunder would resonate loudly in the air. "Wow, that one was close! Only four seconds."

Sean had learned this thunderstorm game from his dad when he was little. It had kept him entertained and not afraid of the storms. So far so good with the girls, as they'd get excited whenever the evening storms came. Nichole would say, "Let's count the thunder."

It seemed like heaven to Kathryn in her summer cottage with Sean, the girls, and the baby. Life was good, and she enjoyed every minute of it.

Chapter Thirty-Five
Gathering Intelligence

Sean had to go to ZAP headquarters for a sales meeting. While he was at the office, he thought it an opportune time to call Dr. Tate and ask about stopping by to see him at his medical practice and maybe getting another round of golf in at Watuppa. He figured it might also be a good way to retrieve any information Dr. Tate might know about the Winslows.

Sean called Dr. Tate's office, and as usual, the secretary took his number and said Dr. Tate would call him when he got a chance. Sean gave her ZAP's office number and his extension and went back to some of his other office work. Not long after the call to Dr. Tate's office, a call came in for Sean. Dr. Tate was returning his call.

"Thanks for calling me back," Sean said. "I was wondering if you'd be around in the near future. I wanted to stop by and update you about some of the trials for Tilamax. It really seems to be working well. Also, I've got some other interesting things coming up that I wanted to discuss with you."

"Yes, Sean," Dr. Tate replied. "Any time during the week is usually okay. Just call the office first and have them set it up."

"Great. Thanks. Oh, and another thing. Are we going to get a chance this summer to get our money back from Dr. Bean and your neighbor, Jim?"

Dr. Tate replied, "Oh, Sean! I guess you haven't heard. Jim Winslow's baby boy, Ryan, was kidnapped."

Oh, my God. You've got to be kidding me! Sean thought. He was momentarily taken aback by the coincidence. He had no idea the baby's name was Ryan when he randomly chose the name for the baby. He took a deep breath and slowly exhaled to regain his composure. "That's awful. When did it happen?"

"Just before Memorial Day," Dr. Tate said with a sigh.

"Wow, when we were last together, Jim's wife hadn't even had the baby yet, and we toasted to the baby."

"Yes, it's just awful."

"I can only imagine. Wow. I have no clue what I'd do if anything ever happened to my girls. Is there any hope they'll get their baby back?"

"They're working with the FBI, but the communications with the kidnapper are going very slowly. They're fairly sure the baby is unharmed and doing well, but there's no word yet on when this nightmare will end."

"God, I'll for sure keep Jim and his family in my thoughts and prayers."

"We all are."

"Well, Dr. Tate, thanks again for returning my call. I'll catch up with you soon. Again, sorry to hear the terrible news about Jim's baby."

"Thanks, Sean. I'll see you soon."

Sean briefly reviewed his conversation with Dr. Tate for any clues to something he may have missed in the conversation. Dr. Tate had said the Winslows felt the baby was unharmed and doing well. This was good. Also, he mentioned that the communications were going slowly. It seemed that Dr. Tate implied that the Winslows were anxious to move this process along; this too was good. All in all, from what he could gather from his conversation with Dr. Tate, everything was going according to his plan, with the exception of the baby having the same name as what he had named the boy. That seemed very weird to Sean.

Chapter Thirty-Six
Ransom Demand

Letter five had arrived. Enclosed was another photo of Ryan, standing, and holding on to a chair covered with a sheet. The background and floor under the chair also were covered by a sheet. The baby had a big grin and looked very happy. These photo shoots were usually quickies. Sean would volunteer to put Ryan down for a nap then quickly place a newspaper next to him.

The quality of the shot was never too important, but fortunately Ryan was a pleasant baby and the photos always showed him looking happy. Letter five, which was two full pages, was the longest letter he'd written the Winslows to date.

Dear Mr. and Mrs. Winslow:

As you can see by this most recent photo, your baby is doing well. As I've mentioned, and as you know, he's a very happy baby. Presently he's cutting a couple of new teeth, but even with that, he fusses very little. He stands all the time now, and I'm sure it won't be long before he begins to walk.

Now it's time to tell you exactly what I want. I will want $1,300,000 (one million three hundred thousand dollars). This will be in used currency. I feel with your family being in the financial world, you won't have any problems securing this amount of cash. Details and instructions will come at a later date, but in the meantime, you may want to start to gather the following denominations of bills:

- seven thousand one-hundred-dollar bills
- seven thousand fifty-dollar bills
- ten thousand twenty-dollar bills
- five thousand ten-dollar bills

Please do not let the FBI convince you to alter the bills in any way or to record the serial numbers. Do not include a GPS device or anything the authorities can trace.

The way this will work is that I will receive the money from you. After I have fully examined the money, I will return your baby to you. This may take some time, but once I'm convinced the money is clean, I will immediately release your baby to you. So again, please be smart. If I even suspect that something isn't to my exact specifications and that the FBI is involved in any way, I will abort the ransom, and you will never see your child again.

You did the normal and right thing by contacting the authorities, but from this point on, they will only slow down the process of your getting your baby back.

As you can see, I am not in a rush. I will take as much time as I feel necessary. When the agents leave your home and stop monitoring your mail, the phones, etc., the process of getting your baby back to you will begin. The choice is yours.

Also, please remember that no matter what the authorities tell you, their primary objective is to apprehend the kidnapper. Your child is certainly important to them but not as important as he is to you and your family. Be smart. Remember, this all boils down to money. The loss of this money is just a transaction or two for you at Winslow and McClure. This should not impact your lives, but not seeing your child again and knowing that someone else is raising him will.

Again, please be smart. Follow my instructions to the T, and you will have your baby home before you know it.

After Molly read the letter, she screamed at Jim, "Get the FBI the hell out of here. I want my baby back. Now! I want them gone now!" Jim tried to put his arm around her, but she flung it off. "I mean it, Jim!" she shouted. "Goddamn it, get rid of them. One point three million is nothing. I'd give them everything we have."

Jim said, "Okay. We'll discuss it, but the FBI is only trying to help."

"Help? What the hell have they done so far? How have they helped? I'm not interested in catching the son of a bitch who took our son. I just want our baby back." Tears rolled down Molly's cheeks as she moved quickly out of the room and up the stairs, continuing her rant, shouting all the louder. "You read the letter. The sooner the FBI is out of here, the sooner we get Ryan back." The bedroom door slammed shut, and then there was silence.

Jim turned to Agent Lacher, who had been standing there, listening to Molly carry on. "I'm sorry about that," Jim said. "All of this has taken its toll on everyone, especially Molly."

Agent Lacher spoke softly. "You know you can't trust a kidnapper. Anyone who would do such a terrible thing isn't beyond lying. This guy, whoever the hell he is, will do anything to get the money. I'm sorry to say that he would put your son in harm's way if it came to it."

"I know you're probably right, but I have to talk to Molly about all of this. Could you guys be a little more low key around here for a while?"

"Certainly. Whatever you say. We're just trying to help."

"I know," Jim said. "Thank you very much for that."

Jim left the agent and walked slowly upstairs. From the hallway, he heard Molly blowing her nose. He felt awful for his wife. As he opened the bedroom door, he said in his most compassionate and soft tone, "Hi, hon. Are you okay?"

Molly walked slowly to him, her eyes full of tears, and placed her head against his shoulder. Jim immediately embraced her and felt the weight of her body leaning into his. "Honey, it'll be okay," he told her. "We'll get our boy back." He closed his eyes, praying earnestly that everything he said would come true.

Molly held Jim tightly, trying hard to compose herself. After a long moment, she said, "Jim, let's sit down and talk."

"Okay."

The master bedroom was quite large and had a sitting area close to a window that looked out toward the southeast side of the house, letting a good amount of morning sunlight into the room. They both took opposite positions on the loveseat, still holding hands and then just fingers as they sat.

Molly was a bit calmer now, even though her eyes were swollen and red from crying. She clutched a tissue in her right hand. "Jim, you read the letter. This guy is only interested in the money. I believe that if we give him what he wants, he'll give us back our son."

Jim rubbed Molly's fingers in a caring and loving way. "I do too, honey, but let's first talk to everyone involved."

"We already did that. They had nothing then, and they have nothing now."

Before Jim could reply, Molly started to break down again, crying. "I'm so sorry for letting the baby out of my sight. I know this is all my fault. I'm so sorry."

Jim slid closer to her, pulling her toward him so her head would rest on his chest. "No, no, no, Molly. This isn't in any way your fault. Some maniac kidnapped our son, and that's it." He paused a moment then continued, "What if you had come back while the kidnapper was taking the baby? God knows what might have happened. Please, let's not go there. It's definitely not your fault."

Molly was just resting her head now, no longer crying. Her husband was kind and caring, and she felt comforted by what he had said—that it wasn't her fault. She picked her head up from Jim's chest, turned, and gave him a kiss. "I love you. I'm trying not to get emotional anymore, but it's so hard for me sometimes."

"I understand." Jim caressed her hair and closed his eyes. "Don't worry. It'll all work out." He thought for a moment. "Well, since we can't communicate with the kidnapper, he has no way of knowing if we're going along with his requests or not, unless there's some other way he knows."

"I wouldn't know how he would know either, but we need to make a decision."

"Okay," Jim said. "But let's please first talk again with everyone involved, give them our point of view, and listen to what they have to say."

Feeling that Jim was now leaning toward her point of view, Molly agreed. "Let's call our parents and get together again with Agent Lacher."

Jim held Molly to him, and once they again embraced. No more words were spoken. They both felt they had gotten what they wanted, but there were no real winners here.

Chapter Thirty-Seven
Vacation Time

Back at the Poconos cottage, Sean was taking one of his vacation weeks. It was now July, and he was enjoying the peace and quiet of the serene mountain getaway. Besides the occasional noise from a car or truck on the nearby road, the only sounds came from nature or the children playing. Sean thought it was great.

That evening while getting ready for bed, Kathryn said, "You know, hon, I haven't even thought of TV, telephone calls, newspapers, or friends. This is unbelievable. I'm totally consumed by this place and the children. Each day blows by, and before you know it, I'm putting the kids in bed and sitting down with a cup of tea and a book for a little quiet time."

"Well, you don't have a cup of tea or a book. What do you want to do with your quiet time tonight?"

Kathryn smiled. "I'm sure I'll think of something."

She turned the light off on the nightstand and rolled over next to Sean. It was pitch black in the room, with only the starlight and a sliver of moonlight filtering through the window. But no light would be needed, as Sean's and Kathryn's touch would provide enough light for the warm lovemaking that was to ensue.

* * *

The next morning after breakfast, Sean had Nichole and Lauren wrapped up in life preservers and settled into the old rowboat at the lake. He was taking his girls for a short boat ride, which they really enjoyed. Every time the boat approached the shoreline, the frogs jumped into the lake, and the girls shouted and pointed.

After the boat ride, Sean and the girls were back at the house, where Kathryn was busy baking cookies in the kitchen. Ever so cute, Ryan was playing quietly in his playpen.

Sean said, "Hey, hon. I'm going back to the office this afternoon for a bit. I need to take care of a few things."

"You're on vacation. Do you have to?"

"Unfortunately I do, but it won't be so bad. I'll be back for dinner. Do you need anything at the store?"

"Yeah, I'll give you a small list."

* * *

Sean got in his car and headed out, but instead of going straight south toward Pennsylvania, he drove east once he got to the I-80 interchange heading toward New York. He had the next letter to mail and needed it to have a New York metro postmark.

As Sean drew close to the George Washington Bridge, he veered off to I-95 south and headed onto the New Jersey Turnpike southbound. When he reached the Port Elizabeth exit, he pulled off and began to look for a mailbox to drop off his next letter to the Winslows.

Perfect, he thought, as he spotted one that was a drive-up. Even though the letter would bear a New Jersey postmark, he was only across the river from Manhattan and next to Staten Island. *This should keep the FBI thinking the kidnapper is still in the New York metro area,* he thought.

Sean finished his drop and headed out to find a grocery store to pick up the items on the list Kathryn had given him. More important, his picking up those items would keep her at home. Before long, Sean had finished his grocery shopping and made his way back to the Poconos for dinner, then hopefully, some bass and crappie fishing on the lake.

Chapter Thirty-Eight
Letters Six, Seven, and Eight

Letters six and seven came a week apart, and each contained a recent photo of the baby looking happy with a *USA Today* beside him, but no correspondence. The important thing was to keep the Winslows feeling confident that Ryan was safe and doing well.

Letter eight was lengthy and contained two photos of the baby. One picture showed the baby standing, not holding on to anything, and the other was the standard photo of the baby next to a recent copy of *USA Today*.

Dear Mr. and Mrs. Winslow:

Check out the photo of your big boy standing on his own. He gets around by crawling, and he can walk by holding on to things. It shouldn't be long before he walks entirely on his own. He remains a very happy baby and is doing quite well.

By now you should have begun to make arrangements to put together the ransom money.

The next item I need you to acquire is a 2008 Chevrolet minivan. I also want you to apply for vanity plates that read any of the following: READY,

RED-D, RID-D, REDDY, Red-D1—any form of the word "ready." From the letters on the license plate, I will know that you have the ransom money.

The ransom money will travel with you everywhere you go, Mrs. Winslow. I want it placed in two separate duffel bags sized to accommodate the bills, with as snug a fit as possible. The bags are to be located on the floor of the backseat, near the sliding side door.

Mrs. Winslow, after you have purchased the minivan, each and every day I want you to drive through town. Travel by the Westchester mall and by the shopping center on Broadway Avenue. You'll get your gas on Main Street across from the Dunkin' Donuts or at the Shell station close to the McDonald's. I want your routine to vary each day.

Now, for sure, this letter will have the FBI jumping for joy, as it gives them more to go on, as well as the possibility of altering the money, recording the serial numbers, planting a GPS device in the money or bags, following your vehicle, placing a GPS monitoring device in your vehicle, and planting agents as workers at the gas stations, McDonald's, Dunkin' Donuts, and the stores. Installing surveillance cameras—even satellite cameras—is their dream.

I advise you again: If you have not yet divorced yourself completely from the FBI and or any other agency that you may have hired or are working with, do so now. As much as they will be looking for me, I will be looking for them. If at any point I feel uncomfortable or feel something isn't right, there absolutely will be no second chance. My correspondence will end immediately, and someone else will raise your baby. For everyone's sake, be smart and do as I have instructed.

With the entire Winslow family present at the Winslow home, along with Molly's mother and father, Special Agent Lacher and Special Agent Haughness reviewed the most recent letter.

Agent Lacher addressed everyone. "The kidnapper is right. We *are* jumping for joy. This is where it all comes together for us. The perp has just given us a blueprint, the means to trap him and follow him to your baby."

Agent Haughness said, "Now the matter about divorcing yourself from the FBI—every kidnapper we've ever investigated demanded the same thing. I want to assure you all that this kidnapper is now playing in our ballpark. We have the best-trained agents in the world. These are true surveillance professionals. We also have the most high-tech monitoring equipment on the planet. With your help we'll capture this man and safely return your child."

Molly fought hard to hold back her emotions. "Agent Lacher, Agent Haughness, I want to thank you both, the other agents, and the FBI for all that you've done on our behalf to date," she said calmly. "But if we look at this practically, all we have to do is give the kidnapper the money and he'll return our child. If we try your method, and he gets wind that you're still working the case, that's the end of the game, and we'll never see Ryan again. My vote and instincts as a mother are to follow the kidnapper's demands."

Agent Lacher looked directly at Jim and his father. "If it were that simple, I'd agree. Just pay the man the money and be done with it. But you're going to put your trust in the man who stole your baby? This man is a deviant and cannot be trusted. What if you give him the money and the correspondence ends? Once this creep has the cash, why would he suddenly get a conscience and take even more risks by returning the baby?

Agent Haughness added, "If that happens, you'll never see Ryan again. With the FBI in place, we'll have the means to capture him and return your child. Please think about it. You're thinking of trusting—please excuse my French—an effing scumbag criminal."

Jim stood up. "Gentlemen, if you wouldn't mind, please allow us to talk about this amongst ourselves."

Looking up, Agent Lacher said, "Sure, Mr. Winslow. We understand. Please do. If I can say one last thing… Please come to your decision using your good judgment and not a decision made purely out of emotion."

After the agents left the room, Jim turned to his family. "Well, guys, what do you think?"

Molly spoke first. She said she felt that the best way to get Ryan back was to do exactly what the kidnapper requested. "I don't trust the kidnapper per se, but he has been consistent with his message of no harm coming to the baby, and he regularly sends us photos. I believe it's really just about the money and that's all he wants."

After a pause, Molly's father spoke up. "After reading the last letter, I feel like this guy has done his homework. If the FBI installs any new surveillance systems noticeable to the public, he'll know it. If they place new employees in the area stores, he'll probably notice someone new, and, as he said, if he even suspects something isn't right, he'll stop the correspondence and we'll never see Ryan again. I'm going with Molly. We're all family and love the baby and want to do the right thing, but there is something to a mother's intuition."

Molly's mother spoke up. "I agree. We should go along with this man's instructions."

Martin Winslow, who was certainly an astute businessman and the head of the Winslow clan, said, "From what I'm told by our company's legal council, the FBI will not ever entirely pull out of this investigation, especially since they've been so involved. We have no say in that, but if we choose to, we don't have to communicate with them any longer."

Jim asked, "Just what are they allowed to do?"

"From what I was told, they can continue without us, acting on the information they already have and anything they gather on their own."

Molly stood up, nervously paced, and in a shaky voice asked, "Do you mean they could try to do things to catch this guy that could screw up the deal, and we could lose the chance to get Ryan back?"

Martin looked at Molly and calmly replied that he believed so, but, first things first, they needed to come to a decision regarding whether they wanted to keep the FBI fully involved.

Molly stopped pacing and faced everyone in the room. She looked each one in the eye and spoke again in a more firm voice. "You all know how I feel. I want to do what the kidnapper says. Let's pay him the bloody money and get Ryan back." She looked at Jim with pleading eyes.

Jim, pretending more confidence than he felt, looked at her. "Okay, dear. I'll go along with your gut feeling and pray that we've made the right decision." He turned to his father. "Can you call any of your connections in Washington to see if they can get the FBI to back off or at least scale down their investigation?"

His father, brow furrowed replied, "I already made those calls, but it was to ask if they could get the FBI to make our case priority one and to put all their resources into it. I guess I could make those same calls again, explain the situation, and ask them to talk to the FBI again. This time I'll have them ask the FBI to back off, or as you put it, at least scale down their investigation, which would limit their exposure."

Jim and Molly thanked everyone, nodding and looking at each other to confirm a united front. With that, everyone else nodded in agreement.

Molly's mother added as she stood up, "I hope and will continue to pray to God that we get Ryan back soon."

"Amen to that," said Mrs. Winslow.

Chapter Thirty-Nine
Political Pull

The next day, Special Agent Lacher received a call from his superior. He was informed that some of the team working with him on the Winslow case would be reassigned elsewhere, as the case seemed not to be progressing and other important FBI cases needed additional help.

After the call, Agent Lacher was speechless. He knew from the recent Winslow family meeting that they had decided to go along with the kidnapper's demands, but even without their cooperation, he still had planned on an extensive surveillance of the listed travel route and also further investigating the money end of the ransom.

One million three hundred thousand dollars wasn't really a lot of money to ask for, considering the risks involved and the wealth of the Winslow family. Why such a small amount? Why the specific amount of one million three hundred thousand? Was this a figure someone had lost dealing in investments with Winslow and McClure?

The FBI already had run a check on disgruntled investors, but Agent Lacher wanted to do some more math in the ransom equation. Perhaps they had overlooked the reasoning behind this exact number or should try to back into this number by looking at what average interest rates would be and then working that number backward to several numbers that someone could have lost. The agent was frustrated. *Now is when I could use extra help*, he thought, and *they're cutting me back.* He figured some higher-ups must have made a call to have them pull back on the case.

Without the necessary manpower, Agent Lacher would be unable to have a complete surveillance team. He set up a meeting with his few remaining team members and told them, "This case has been put on the back burner. I've been told that the Winslows formally requested that we not have any further discussions with them. Without the family's cooperation and by losing the balance of our team, all we can do is continue to follow up on our existing leads. For now we won't be able to pursue any new leads without direct consent from my superior." Agent Lacher looked disgusted. "In other words we must keep our distance from the Winslows. Someone with big-time clout has more than likely pressured the higher-ups to back off."

Agent Lacher was thinking he knew who that must have been.

Chapter Forty
The Travel Route

With Sean's vacation week over, he was back at home alone in Pennsylvania, catching up on a week's worth of work and lining up appointments for that week. He also needed to observe the route he had instructed Molly to travel each day. He didn't feel she would have gotten everything ready yet—the vanity license plates, the minivan, and the denominations of bills—but, as he had mentioned in his letter, he would now be looking for signs of the FBI's presence.

Sean thought this might also be a good time to stop by and see Dr. Tate, per their recent discussion. Perhaps Dr. Tate may have a bit more information. Sean got the appointment set up, and the next morning, he was up early, traveling to visit with him.

Sean pulled into the parking lot of Westchester Medical Center and then waited in Dr. Tate's office while the doctor was seeing patients. It wasn't too long before Dr. Tate came in with an apology for having kept him waiting.

"No problem," Sean said. "I was just happy that you could take a few minutes to see me."

"Oh, I always have time for you, young man. What do you have going on?"

Sean reviewed some new literature put out by ZAP and discussed how well the Tilamax trials had been going. He also had some literature to leave with the doctor about other new drugs ZAP was working on, but these were a long ways off compared to Tilamax. Within the year, ZAP was hoping to have the trials for Tilamax completed so it could get the FDA's final review and approval.

As the brief meeting was ending, Sean said, "Say, Dr. Tate, how are the Winslows? Have they been able to get their baby back yet?"

Dr. Tate grew solemn. "I'm afraid not, but I recently spoke with Jim, and he said things look promising. In a short amount of time, they may have their child back. At least I hope so."

"Yes, me too."

* * *

Back in the car, Sean tried to analyze everything Dr. Tate had said.

Let's see, thought Sean. *Dr. Tate spoke recently with Jim Winslow. Jim told him things looked promising and that they might get their baby back soon. That's great.* He started the engine and drove along, looking for the lane to merge onto the road that would take him to Rye. *The fact that the Winslows told Dr. Tate this means they probably are going along with all demands. This news is good, very good*, thought Sean.

Sean reached the town of Rye, taking the route he had instructed Molly to drive each day. He pretended to be casually driving, but he looked at all the telephone poles, buildings, and surrounding landscape to see whether any cameras were visible and to note where each was located. That way he would later know whether anything new had been installed. He also checked local stores to see whether they had any cameras, in which direction they were pointed, and how much of an area they could cover. He was sure that later, if the FBI wanted to, they could conceal themselves very well, but for now he was observing what was obvious to him and in plain sight. The hub of his plan was still based on his getting Molly Winslow to trust him enough to push the Winslow clan to either get the FBI off the case or get it downgraded in importance. Sean felt that in the not-too-distant future, if he kept up the correspondence, the Winslows would fully cooperate with his plan. What he didn't know was that they already had accepted his conditions and planned to go along with his demands.

Sean's drive didn't reveal much, but he really hadn't expected to see anything. He merely wanted to familiarize himself with the surroundings.

Chapter Forty-One
Nancy's Letter

Near sundown on Friday, Sean arrived at the cottage for the weekend. He gave Kathryn a new letter from Nancy.

> Dear Kathryn and Sean,
>
> Please forgive me for not writing earlier, but the rehab job-training center is very tight with rules and strict on policy. To be able to even see visitors or make or receive phone calls, you have to earn points. At first I had a little trouble adjusting, but now I'm on track and doing well.
>
> I've been saving my points so that when Sean comes up to Massachusetts on one of his sales trips, I'll have earned enough points to see him. Sean, I hope you'll have time to see me next time you come up to Fall River.
>
> I hope my little angel Ryan hasn't been too much trouble for either of you. He is my motivation here. I think of him every day.

Please write back and let me know how he is, and if you could send me a recent photo, I'd really appreciate it. My address is on the envelope.

Thanks again, guys. I owe you both big time.

All my love,

Nancy

Kathryn teared up just reading the letter. "Oh, that poor girl! I don't know that I could ever stand to be away from Nichole and Lauren for three months. I'm going to write to her tomorrow."

"That would be nice. I'll take a couple of pictures of Ryan for you to include in your letter."

"I'm sure she'd love that."

The return address on the envelope was Nancy Robinson, C/O FRRC, PO Box 24351, Fall River, MA 02720. This was a PO Box Sean had set up in Fall River months ago. The addressee didn't matter to the post office; the only thing that mattered was the box number in the address. Also, no mail sent there would ever be returned to the sender.

Chapter Forty-Two
Letters Nine and Ten

Letters nine and ten arrived a week apart. Again, Sean didn't mention anything in either letter about the ransom or anything to do with the kidnapping. He included a photo of Ryan with each letter along with a little quip about how well the baby was doing.

Molly treasured each photo of the baby. She placed them all in order, and every day she sat and gazed at her boy, pointing out to Jim each and every little detail that showed how the baby was growing.

After receiving the latest correspondence, Molly took out the other photos again, noting any obvious changes in the baby. She called Jim over. "Look. Here's a photo of Ryan from June, and now look at the newest photo. He's losing some of his baby fat."

Jim caressed her hair and face. "I see, hon. Hopefully it won't be long before we have our angel back."

Molly held the photos in one hand and touched Jim's arm with the other. She nodded, trying to hold back tears, and softly said, "Yes, hopefully it won't be too long."

Chapter Forty-Three
The Waiting Game

It was now August, three weeks since the Winslows had received Sean's letter with his instructions and demands. Sean felt by now that the Winslows probably had gotten the minivan and should have all the cash ready. He would continue to go out of his way on a couple of his sales trips to swing by the town of Rye on the chance of seeing Mrs. Winslow driving the van with the "ready" license plate. So far he hadn't seen the minivan. Sean would make a pass through town on his way north and then again on his way south. In addition to not seeing the minivan, Sean hadn't spotted any obvious new cameras. This, he thought, was good. He also felt pretty secure that in a short amount of time he eventually would see the minivan and Mrs. Winslow. However, what would he do if he didn't see the minivan before the summer rental ended. What then?

A knot formed in his stomach at the thought. *What the hell will I do if I don't see the van?* he wondered. He would only have a limited number of times when he could actually get to Rye, and he also didn't want to be constantly driving around town. What were his options? This was a tough deal for him, as everything so far had been perfect. This potential scenario could be disastrous to the whole plan.

What the hell will I do? played over and over in Sean's mind. *We certainly can't take the baby back home with us. Too many neighbors will see him, and then the questions will come.* The rest of the day and into the evening, Sean pondered the dilemma until he thought, *If by the end of the rental, I haven't seen the mini-van, I'll return the baby as I'd planned. All will have been for nothing, but at least I won't get caught and no harm will have come to the baby.* With this last thought, he felt at least he had a plan. He still felt, however, that he eventually would see the minivan and Mrs. Winslow, and everything would work out.

Besides taking her daily drives through town, to the mall, and to shopping center, the first thing Molly did each day was to stop by the post office to check her mail before it went out with the local mailman. She wanted to get the mail right away in case there was any correspondence from the kidnapper. She also wanted to be the first one to get the mail because the Winslows were no longer cooperating with the FBI. In fact, Molly had told Jim she felt so much better knowing the FBI was no longer intercepting their personal mail.

Chapter Forty-Four
Letter Eleven

When Molly received the eleventh letter, she quickly exited the post office, got into the minivan, and drove to the far end of the parking lot. There she carefully sliced open the envelope.

Mr. and Mrs. Winslow:

As you can see from the enclosed photo, Ryan is growing like a weed, and from the photo, you'll also notice that he's walking on his own. He started just the other day and hasn't stopped since. He's doing very well.

Mrs. Winslow, continue with your daily drives, and please be patient, as this process may take some time.

The letter was brief and to the point, but the picture spoke a thousand words. Ryan was standing, and Molly could tell he was about to take his first step. She flipped opened her cell phone and called Jim. She read him the letter and described the photo. In a teary voice she said, "I can feel it. We're getting closer to getting Ryan back."

Jim tried to be reassuring despite his fears. "Yes, honey. I feel it too."

Later, back at home, Molly would, as she often did, reread all the kidnapper's correspondence and look at all the photos the kidnapper had sent. Looking at the photos of Ryan in progression, she thought, *He's right. My sweet baby Ryan is growing like a weed. Oh, God! I miss him so much.*

Chapter Forty-Five
Summer's End

It was mid-August, and Labor Day was fast approaching. Kathryn said to Sean, "This has been the best summer vacation ever! Thank you so much for doing this."

"Hey," Sean said. "I've loved it too."

"You know, it'll be hard for me to give back Ryan. I've grown so fond of him. He's been such a great baby."

"All the kids are asleep. Maybe we could try to come up with our own baby Ryan."

"Well, he certainly has made it easy for me to go along with the idea."

"Want to give it the old college try?"

"Gee, Sean," Kathryn said. "You're so romantic! That's nice, sweet talk, 'the old college try.' "

"Oh, come on. I'm always romancing you."

"Mmmm," Kathryn said, with a sly little smirk.

Chapter Forty-Six
RIDD4U

The next morning was the start of the new week. Sean had set up business plans to head north into Connecticut. This, of course, gave him another reason to swing by Rye to see whether he could spot the minivan and Mrs. Winslow.

It had rained earlier that morning. Dark clouds loomed overhead, and there was little to no sunlight; the streets were still wet with puddles. Because of the slick driving conditions, traffic on the main road was a bit slower that day. As Sean drove by the town's shopping center, he saw a minivan stopped at the light in the turn lane headed into the shopping center. The license plate read, RIDD4U. *Oh, my God*, he thought. Instantly his heartbeat went into overdrive—just like the day he had kidnapped the baby. What to do now? Was it show time? The signal turned green, allowing the cars in the turn lane to enter the shopping center. Sean glanced at the driver. She was a female and looked to be Mrs. Winslow. He wasn't 100 percent sure, but who else could it be, an undercover FBI agent? *No*, thought Sean. *That would blow the whole deal for the Winslows if the kidnapper happened to know what Mrs. Winslow looks like.* It had to be her.

The traffic light changed and allowed him to drive past the shopping center, take the first left, and enter the parking lot from the side street. As Sean drove into the parking lot, he saw Mrs. Winslow get out of her car and head into grocery store. *Good*, Sean thought. *This'll give me a little bit of time to get ready.*

He drove around to the side lot of the shopping center, out of sight of the main parking lot, where he parked his car. In a zipped bag in the backseat, he had a lightweight pullover sweatshirt. He also had a stick-on mustache, sunglasses, and a baseball cap—all of which would give him a Unabomber look. He didn't think the disguise would completely conceal his looks, but it would give him enough of a different look that it would be tough for Mrs. Winslow to get a true image of him. *Better than nothing*, he thought. He also was wearing his skin-toned, ultra-lightweight fishing gloves.

As he exited his car, he pulled out from under his car seat the two stolen Rhode Island license plates he had affixed to his vehicle the day he had kidnapped Ryan. He walked to the rear of his car and attached one of the magnetic plates. Then, nonchalantly, he walked to the front of the vehicle and carefully looked to see whether he was being noticed by anyone. He didn't see anyone watching him, so he popped on the other plate.

Sean walked to the main parking lot, past Mrs. Winslow's minivan, to a trashcan a couple of rows away. He reached into his sweatshirt pocket and removed a manila envelope addressed to Mrs. Winslow. He dropped the envelope into the trashcan and walked away. He was truly on adrenaline overdrive now. His heart pounded so hard that he felt his chest moving. *Calm down*, he told himself. *Just be calm*. He walked in the direction of the nearby McDonald's. As he walked, he watched the supermarket entrance. *There she is*, he thought. *It's show time.*

As Molly Winslow walked to the minivan, pushing her grocery cart, Sean turned around and headed toward the minivan as well. He was timing his pace to arrive at the vehicle a moment or two after Mrs. Winslow got there.

Mrs. Winslow pulled her shopping cart next to the rear door and opened the minivan's back hatch. As she turned to retrieve her grocery bags from the cart, she was startled to see a man standing next to her. "Mrs. Winslow, please be calm. I've come to take your minivan."

With that, he reached into the shopping cart and took out one of the bags, as if he were helping her put the bag into the back of the minivan. Molly's hands were shaking, and she started to ask, "Do you have my Ryan?"

Sean interrupted her. "Mrs. Winslow, are you being followed?"

"No."

"Are there any monitoring devices in the van or with the money?"

"Absolutely not. I insisted on doing everything you asked."

Sean continued, "Is the money in the van, and is it used and non-traceable?"

"Yes, we've done everything you asked us to do. When can we get our baby back?"

Sean put the last bag of groceries into the rear of the minivan and said, "Mrs. Winslow, I'll need your car keys. Do you see that trashcan secured to the lamp post over there?"

Molly turned to look. "Yes."

Sean said, "Inside the trash can is a manila envelope with instructions. If everything is okay with the money, you'll soon have your son returned to you. Please be calm. Again, if everything is okay, you'll have your baby back soon."

Molly reached into her purse and handed Sean her keys. Sean turned, slammed the rear hatch shut, and without saying another word, walked to the driver's side of the van. Molly had so much to say and so much to ask, but she just watched Sean get into her minivan and drive off. As the vehicle pulled away, she walked briskly toward the trash container. There, just as Sean had said, was a manila envelope with her name on it. She pulled out the envelope, opened it, and removed the letter.

Mrs. Winslow:

If everything is okay with the money, I'll let you know where you can pick up your son. Please be patient. This shouldn't take long, but I must first be sure everything is all right. You should call your husband and have him pick you up.

Molly's body felt limp as she leaned against the light post. She felt a bit lightheaded, but in short order, she calmed down, gained her composure, and took out her cell phone. With her hands a bit jittery, she called her husband.

After Jim answered, she said, "I'm at the grocery store in the shopping center. The kidnapper came and took my minivan."

Jim asked, "Are you okay? What happened? Did you see what he looked like?"

Molly said firmly, "I don't give a shit what he looked like. He came up to me when I was about to put the groceries into the minivan and asked me to be calm. He asked if everything was as he'd instructed. I told him yes. He asked for my keys and told me to go to a trashcan, where there would be another letter."

"Did you get the letter? What did it say?"

"It said if everything was okay with the money, we'd get Ryan back shortly. Jim, come get me."

"Okay, honey," Jim said. "Stay calm. I'm on my way."

Molly told Jim she'd meet him in the coffee shop next to the grocery store and to hurry.

"I'm already walking to my car," he told her. "I'll be there as fast as I can." He ended the conversation by saying, "Molly, you did great. I love you."

"I love you too."

Chapter Forty-Seven
I'm a Millionaire

Sean drove around to the side of the parking lot and pulled up next to his car so that the minivan's sliding doors were next to the driver's side of his car. He walked around to the sliding door and opened it. The two duffel bags were on the floor of the backseat. He grabbed one of them and opened the rear door of his vehicle and flung the bag inside. He did the same with the second bag. He closed the minivan's side door, jumped into his car, and calmly drove off.

Holy shit, Sean thought. *If I don't die of a heart attack right now, I'm a millionaire. I did it! I did it! Holy shit. I did it.*

Sean kept his cool, not wanting to break any traffic laws and get pulled over. He drove very cautiously for the next few miles then turned onto I-95 south. Just a few miles down the road was a rest stop area. He pulled in, removed the Rhode Island plates from his car, and placed the two bags of cash into the trunk. When he placed the bags in the trunk, he opened one of them, exposing the cash. The urge to take some of it out was overwhelming, but his desire to stick to his plan kept him from doing so.

Back on I-95 south, he headed to his home in Pennsylvania. He prayed there wouldn't be any traffic jams like the time he had driven the baby home. If that happened again, he felt he would surely croak.

Chapter Forty-Eight
It's Almost Over

Jim Winslow pulled into the shopping center parking lot, close to where the coffee shop was. Before he could get to the coffee shop, Molly walked out and headed quickly toward Jim and the car. Jim got out of his car and took a few steps, extending his arms and pulling Molly toward him. He held her tightly and whispered, "We're almost there, honey. Soon we'll have Ryan back."

Molly pressed her head against Jim's chest. She felt his heart thumping as tears puddled in her eyes. The two of them stayed there, glued to each other for what felt like hours. After a minute or two, Jim said in a soft voice, "Come on. Let's go home. We'll call our parents from there." Jim walked her to the passenger side of the car and opened the door for her and helped her in. As they drove home, Molly again relayed everything that had happened and read the kidnapper's letter to Jim again.

"Please," she said. "Tell me that we did everything he asked us to."

"Yes, we did everything he asked us to do. Now he needs to keep his promise and return our son."

"He was right in front of me, but I didn't want to look at him too much. I was afraid he might think I was trying to identify him."

"You did the right thing. You handled it perfectly. I'm sure he'll return Ryan to us."

As they headed home, Jim drove with his left hand on the steering wheel and held Molly's hand with his right hand. Their fingers wrapped together as they both prayed that soon they would have their baby back.

Chapter Forty-Nine
My Turn to Worry

Sean continued to drive on I-95 south with his car on cruise control a couple of miles below the speed limit. No way did he want his excitement and adrenaline to get him pulled over. Paranoia had begun to set in. He didn't want to let it into his head, but many troubling thoughts entered his mind. *Shit*, he thought. *What the hell do I do if the money is tainted or traceable or if there's some kind of a James Bond GPS device tucked into the bundles of money or the duffel bags? Damn. Now it's my turn to worry.*

He pulled into his driveway and hit the automatic garage door opener. Once the garage door closed behind him, he took the two bags from the car and went down to his clean room to go through everything. *Hell*, he thought. *I have twenty-nine thousand bills to look at, plus the bags themselves. Oh, God. This is going to take quite a while.*

Sean quickly removed the money from the bags. He needed to see whether any GPS devices were attached to the bag or hidden in the stitching. He went right to work, going through both bags, tearing them apart, destroying them in the process. *Good, nothing there*, he thought, *Now the packets of bills*. He was concerned there could be a GPS device hidden in the stacks of bills themselves. He cut each packet of bills open and thumbed through all of them. This went on long into the night, which kept his mind busy so he wouldn't think too much about what may have gone wrong.

As the time passed, Sean became more confident that the Winslows had done everything he had asked them to do and that everything was clean. *Now let's see if I can go to sleep*, he thought as he headed upstairs to his bedroom.

Chapter Fifty
Stash the Cash

With a big grin the next morning, Sean thought, *Well, don't give up your day job!* He made some work calls from his house, making sure he was covering himself on the business side of things. By midmorning, he was all set with his business and headed back down to the basement to begin restacking the money.

His plan was to keep one hundred thousand dollars hidden well in his basement. He'd wrap the other one million two hundred thousand tightly in waterproof shrink-wrap. Then he'd place the wrapped bundles of cash into two very large Tupperware containers. He'd wrap these containers in the same shrink-wrap so they'd be completely airtight and waterproof.

In the Pocono Mountains, not far from the cottage he'd rented, Sean had dug two deep holes in which to bury the containers of money. He had dug these holes while he was there earlier on his week's vacation. He figured he could leave the cash there until he found a more suitable place to hide it, which would give him better access to it.

After he had the one hundred thousand securely hidden in his basement, he packed the two wrapped Tupperware containers in the trunk of his car and headed toward the cottage to bury them. Once he completed his task, he'd drive the few more miles to the cottage where Kathryn and the girls would be.

The hiding spot for the cash was just off a side road that seemed not to be used very much. He could back up to the holes, which were camouflaged just in case someone happened to stumble on them.

After arriving at the hiding spot, he quickly took each container from the trunk of his car and dropped them into the two holes. He picked up the shovel and rake he had left under the camo covering and began to fill up the holes, burying the two containers.

After Sean covered everything up, he raked the area smooth and covered the exposed dirt with leaves and forest debris. By the time he was done, no one would be able to tell that anything was buried there. Satisfied with the job, he took off his dirty, sweaty clothes and put on a pair of fresh trousers and a clean shirt. *I can't go back to the cottage looking like a gravedigger,* he thought. After he finished slicking himself up, he got back into his car and drove to the main road.

Chapter Fifty-One
Say Goodbye to Ryan

Not long after, Sean pulled up to the cottage. Kathryn was outside with the children and was surprised to see him. "Hey, there!" she said. "Are you playing hooky again?"

Sean laughed. "Sort of."

He walked over to Nichole and Lauren, who were making their way to him, yelling, "Daddy's here!"

He looked over at Kathryn again. "I have some really good news and some bad news."

Kathryn said, "Oh, crap! Give me the bad news first and get it over with."

"Okay. I'm taking Ryan back to Nancy tomorrow."

"Oh, no," Kathryn groaned. "I'm going to miss him so much! Can the girls and I come with you?"

Shaking his head, Sean quickly came up with an excuse. "Sorry, dear. You were right. I am playing hooky from work. I have to make all kinds of sales calls on my way back to cover my ass."

By this time the girls had placed themselves on each of Sean's feet, getting a ride on the lawn, while he walked and talked to Kathryn. With the girls on each foot, he leaned over to Kathryn and gave her a quick smooch. "Say, where is the little guy?"

"On the blanket there." She pointed to a blanket next to a shade tree.

"Oh, he is a darling one," said Sean. "I'm going to miss him too."

Kathryn said, "Okay. So give me the good news."

"The good news is that normally Nancy would be graduating from her program in a couple of weeks, but a job opening came up at a daycare center, and her counselor recommended her for it."

"That's great. That's just wonderful."

"Yeah, it's a dream job for her. She'll be able to work and take care of Ryan at the same time. So, as you can imagine, she called me right away and asked if I could bring Ryan back to her as soon as I could. I was so excited for her that I turned around and drove all the way back here. I plan on bringing Ryan back to her first thing tomorrow."

"That's why I love you—because you're so thoughtful." Kathryn circled her arms around his waist, and they kissed again. "Well, then you'd better watch the children and let me start putting all of Ryan's things together."

"Okay, I'll get some bread and let the girls feed the bluegills and sunnies down at the pond."

"That'll keep them busy. Just keep an eye on the baby when you do."

"No problem. He looks like he'll be out for a while."

Chapter Fifty-Two
Anticipation

Jim and Molly were at home, nervously awaiting any news from the kidnapper about getting Ryan back. Jim had assured Molly a thousand times that he hadn't conspired with the FBI in regard to the money or any tracing devices. Everything had been done exactly as the kidnapper had requested.

"Then we should be hearing from him soon," Molly said.

"Yes." Jim tried reassure her that everything would be okay. "You do realize that it may take a little while for the kidnapper to check things out."

"I know. I'm just so anxious because we did everything he asked us to do."

"I'm sure once he checks things out and sees that everything is okay, we'll get Ryan back."

"Okay," Molly said. "Let's call our parents and tell them the good news."

Molly called her mother while Jim called his father. They both reviewed the details of Molly's encounter with the kidnapper and what the letter had said. All parties agreed that it shouldn't be long before the kidnapper returned Ryan. It was a little too early to celebrate, but good feelings abounded with the Winslows and Sullivans.

Chapter Fifty-Three
Mrs. Brown

Early the next morning, Sean loaded up his car with all of Ryan's things. Kathryn had fed and changed the baby and prepared his juice and snacks for his trip back to his mother.

"Ask Nancy to write us with pictures of Ryan. Does she have a computer and e-mail?"

"Not yet," Sean said as he fit in the last package of diapers. "She'll be busy for a while, getting back on her feet. Once she does, I'm sure she'll write."

Sean figured he'd send another couple of letters from Nancy, then just let things fade from there, saying, "Oh, well. That's Nancy." Also, with no reason for Kathryn to be going to Fall River, the chances of her ever meeting Nancy were slim to none.

"Well, send her our love and tell her congratulations on completing her program and getting the new job."

"I will."

Sean strapped Ryan into the car seat, and Kathryn and the girls got their last smooches and hugs from Ryan. Sean kissed the girls and Kathryn and drove off, watching them all wave goodbye. He glanced over his shoulder at Ryan, who was playing with a big cookie. "Well, little guy, it's time to get you back to your real mom and dad."

Sean drove down the mountain to the Delaware River. Instead of his usual route, south to the Delaware Water Gap and I-80, he turned north, traveling along the river up to I-84 east, headed across New York State and into Danbury, Connecticut, which was less than an hour north of the Winslows' home.

The town of Danbury is a typical New England community, with older, three-story tenement homes, a large Catholic cathedral, and corner taverns for the blue-collar factory and construction workers. When Sean pulled into town, he stopped at a phone booth next to a small laundry facility called Soap & Suds. He pulled out a slip of newspaper from his wallet that read, "Child Care: Will babysit in my own home. Call 362-0129."

Sean dialed the number. "Hi. Mrs. Brown? This is James Wynn. I spoke to you the other day."

"Oh, yes," she said. "How are you?"

"Fine, Mrs. Brown. I had something come up this morning that's going to keep me busy all afternoon, and I was hoping you could watch my son, Ryan, for me."

"Yes," said Mrs. Brown. "That would be fine. Just bring along anything you think he'll need, and I'll take care of him from there."

"Okay, thanks," said Sean. "If you can give me directions to your house, I'll come right over."

After getting the directions, Sean hung up the phone, took off his gloves, and got back into the car. He proceeded directly to Mrs. Brown's place. When Sean found her house, he drove about half a block past it and parked. Before he got out of the car, he put on his sunglasses and a baseball cap, but he didn't bother with the fake mustache this time. He went over to the passenger side door, picked up Ryan, and grabbed his diaper bag with all the necessities that Kathryn had packed away for him. He had been careful to wipe everything clean. "Okay, big guy," said Sean. "You're almost home."

Sean used a large baby cloth to handle the bag's shoulder strap, then slung it over his shoulder and scooped up Ryan.

He walked up to Mrs. Brown's front door. The small white house appeared well kept even though the porch looked like it could use a new coat of paint. Beautiful annuals in riotous colors framed the front of the porch. Before Sean could ring the bell, the door opened and a cheerful voice greeted him. "Hi," said Mrs. Brown.

"Hi. I'm James Wynn, and this is Ryan. Nice to meet you."

"And you too. Here. Let me help you with the baby."

Mrs. Brown looked to be in her mid- to late sixties and more than likely was already on Social Security and was babysitting to earn extra pocket cash.

She had a very pleasant face and looked like she had just walked out of a Norman Rockwell painting of a grandmother at a Thanksgiving table. Sean passed the baby to Mrs. Brown with no fuss from him whatsoever. Ryan looked at her and smiled as if he had known her his whole life.

"Oh, he's a friendly little boy," she said, giving the baby a peck on his chubby cheek.

"Yes, he is. Mrs. Brown, here in the side pouch of the diaper bag is contact information for my wife, Molly, in case you should need to get a hold of us."

"Good," she replied, ushering Sean into the house. "What time do you think you'll be coming back for Ryan?"

"Oh, somewhere close to five," Sean answered, placing the baby bag on the floor by the door.

"That'll be just fine."

"Well, Mrs. Brown, I can't tell you how much I appreciate your being able to watch Ryan on such short notice."

"No problem, Mr. Wynn," she said. "You have a good day. I'm sure Ryan and I will do the same."

As Sean scampered down the porch steps, he turned and shouted back, waving his hand, "Thanks again, Mrs. Brown."

As he made his way onto the sidewalk, he heard the front door to Mrs. Brown's house close shut.

Chapter Fifty-Four
Hi, Is James There?

Sean drove out of Danbury and toward Bridgeport, Connecticut, to begin making sales calls. As he drove, he thought, *Well, you did it. You're now a true millionaire. Everything went according to plan, no one was physically hurt, and now you have a major head start on a wonderful life.* For the next half-hour, he couldn't stop grinning, thinking of all the possibilities and all the things he could do now that he had the money.

* * *

When five thirty and then six p.m. rolled by, Mrs. Brown began to worry a bit about James Wynn being late. She pulled out the contact information he had left for her in the pouch on the side of the diaper bag. The note listed a telephone number for Jim and Molly Wynn. Mrs. Brown picked up her phone and dialed the number, and the phone rang at the Winslows' home. Jim had gone to the country club to have dinner with clients, and Molly was home alone. She picked up the phone.

Mrs. Brown said, "Hi. This is Mrs. Brown. Is James there?"

Molly answered, "No, this is Molly. I'm James's wife. May I help you?"

"Yes, your husband, James, dropped off your baby, Ryan, here today for me to watch. He said he'd be back around five, but he hasn't come by yet. Do you know if he's on his way?"

Molly nearly fell to the floor, her face flushed with nervousness. "Mrs. Brown," she said, "did you say you're watching my son, Ryan, right now?"

"Yes," replied Mrs. Brown. "He's a lovely child."

"Oh, God, Mrs. Brown! Where are you? How do I get to you?"

Mrs. Brown sensed something wasn't right. The woman on the other end sounded distraught. "Mrs. Wynn, are you all right? Is something wrong?"

Molly was almost in tears as she blurted, "Mrs. Brown, my name is Molly Winslow, not Wynn. Our baby, Ryan, was kidnapped three months ago."

"Oh, my!" said Mrs. Brown, placing a hand on her chest, not quite believing what she'd heard.

"Yes," said Molly. "We recently paid the kidnapper the ransom he asked for and were waiting for the return of our child."

Mrs. Brown said, "Well, the baby I have here is a boy about nine to ten months old. He has blond hair and blue eyes."

"Mrs. Brown!" cried Molly. "That's our son, Ryan! That's my baby."

Molly started to cry. Mrs. Brown, hearing her, consoled her and assured her everything would be okay. When Molly calmed down, she was able to get Mrs. Brown's phone number, address, and directions to her home.

Mrs. Brown asked if she should call the police. "Not now, please," Molly said. "We'll call them when we get there. Oh, God bless you, Mrs. Brown," she said, as tears rolled down her cheeks again.

The moment Molly hung up the phone, she hit the speed dial for her husband's cell phone. Jim answered the phone while backing away from the table where he was sitting with his clients.

He had barely answered when Molly said, "Jim, we have Ryan back."

Jim gasped. "We do? What? When?"

"He is at a babysitter's house in Danbury, Connecticut. The lady watching him, Mrs. Brown, just called me." She took a deep breath, but it did little to slow the torrent of words. "Jim, come right now! I'm so excited I'm shaking."

"I'll be right there."

Jim quickly excused himself from his clients, saying he needed to attend to a family matter but would call them first thing in the morning. The clients knew about Jim's kidnapped son and assumed his leaving had something to do with that. "Sure, Jim," they told him. "We're fine. You take care of whatever you need to do."

Jim was home in a flash and found Molly waiting outside. She had her cell phone to her ear and was talking to her mother. As Jim pulled up, he heard her say, "Okay, Mom. Jim's here. I'll call you when we get Ryan. Bye."

As Molly opened the car door, she and Jim were like two lovers who hadn't seen each other in a long time. Molly came busting into the car with her knees on the seat. She wrapped her arms around Jim's neck and squeezed him tightly. "We have him back! We have him back!" she cried, as her tears of joy began to flow.

Chapter Fifty-Five
The Nightmare Ends

On the drive to Danbury, Jim was able to call Mrs. Brown again to confirm everything and to let her know they were on their way. He also called his mother and father to tell them the good news. All the family members would be waiting for Jim and Molly when they returned home with the baby.

As Jim neared Mrs. Brown's house, he thought it prudent to contact Special Agent Lacher to let him know they were picking up the baby. When Jim made the call, Agent Lacher advised him that another agent would meet him there shortly and that this wouldn't impede or delay their taking their son home.

Agent Lacher ended the conversation by congratulating Jim and Molly on the return of their baby. He added that he would personally stop by first thing in the morning to see them.

"There it is, Jim. Nine thirteen High Street, a white, two-story house."

Jim pulled up to the curb, with Molly opening the car door, not waiting for Jim. She exited the car and dashed up the stairs to the woman on the porch, who was holding a little boy on her hip.

As Molly moved across the sidewalk and up the stairs, Mrs. Brown placed Ryan on the porch. He was standing all on his own. Molly moved forward and fell to her knees, her arms extended in front of her baby boy. Molly didn't know whether he could still remember her after three months— or maybe he was just being the pleasant boy he was— but Ryan took a couple of steps and entered his mother's waiting arms. Molly nearly smothered the baby with hugs, kisses, and tears.

Jim stood behind her and said with a joyous chuckle, "Hey, kiddo! Let him breathe."

Molly and Mrs. Brown, who had a tissue up to her eyes, laughed. Jim got down on one knee, and said, "Hey, my big boy. Come give Daddy a hug." As Jim hugged his son, Molly looked into his eyes and neither had to say a word. The nightmare finally was over.

Chapter Fifty-Six
Keeping Cool

Sean had worked his way over to New Haven, Connecticut, and was staying at the Marriott just off I-95. He was having dinner and a beer in the lounge at the bar, watching his favorite team, the Boston Red Sox, on the flat-screen TV located behind the bar. This was a great day for Sean. He had pulled off the perfect crime. *Yes*, he thought. *I planned everything well, stuck to my plan, and executed everything perfectly.* He thought tonight he was deserving of a few cold beers.

Tomorrow, Sean planned to make more sales calls. He would then head back to Pennsylvania to the cottage to take his second vacation week with his family, but right now he was enjoying a cold beer, watching the Sox beat the Yankees, and feeling good—very good indeed.

Chapter Fifty-Seven
Back to Suburbia

Labor Day weekend came, which ended the Murphys' summer vacation. Kathryn had loved every minute of the peace and solitude at the cottage—just her, the children, and Sean, whenever he could be there. It had been the best summer ever. Now it would be back home to suburbia and a more hectic schedule with the children's activities, the house, friends, and Sean.

After putting the girls to sleep, Kathryn began to pack up. Sean called out, "Hey, we have all day tomorrow to do that. This is our last night here. Get your sweet little buns over here." Kathryn looked over at Sean, who was on the couch, with the fireplace lit. Sean held out a glass of chilled wine.

"Now that's romantic," Kathryn said, as she moved toward the couch, taking the wineglass from Sean's hand. She took a sip and scooted onto the couch next to her hubby.

"See? I do know how to woo you."

Kathryn held the glass away from both of them and moved in closer for a kiss.

Chapter Fifty-Eight
Picnic

The Winslows were having a wonderful Labor Day picnic celebration, with the extended Winslow and Sullivan families in attendance. It was a happy time once again, and everyone's spirits were high with the excitement of Molly and Jim getting their baby back.

Master Ryan James Winslow was certainly the toast of the party, receiving hugs and kisses from all who attended. Someone commented, "The poor baby's feet have hardly hit the ground all day, going from one person to another." This was true, as everyone wanted to hold, hug, and kiss the precious little boy.

The end of summer drifted into autumn, and soon the colorful fall bled into winter. Molly was once again happy, decorating her home for Christmas and for Santa's arrival. The horrid summer was over and although not forgotten, it was put back, way back, in the Winslows' minds. To dwell on those horrible few months would do no one any good.

Molly's only thoughts now of those awful summer months were of how she, Jim, and their family were united in love and prayer. It wasn't that they hadn't already loved and been close to one another; it was just that the entire emotional episode seemed to permanently fuse them all together. This is what Molly wanted to take out of what had happened.

Chapter Fifty-Nine
Bonus Time

Back in Pennsylvania, Sean was priming the pump, planting more seeds, with hints to Kathryn that he might be getting a decent bonus for Christmas—enough, say, to maybe go on a nice vacation to Florida with the kids.

Kathryn was very excited with the possibility. "If anyone deserves a raise and bonus, you do," she said. "Heck, you worked your butt off with road trips all summer. I'll keep my fingers crossed."

Sean smiled. "Yeah, all those road trips may have paid off. I've got it from a pretty reliable source that I'll be more than pleased."

Chapter Sixty
Merry Christmas

Santa came to the Murphy house on Christmas Eve. In the morning, when the children awoke, Kathryn and Sean heard the girls rush down the decorated hallway to the master bedroom, yelling, "Merry Christmas! Merry Christmas! Mommy, Daddy! Merry Christmas!"

"Let's go," Kathryn said to Nichole. "Let's see what Santa brought us."

"Hey," Sean said. "Don't we get Merry Christmas kisses and hugs first?" Nichole and Lauren scurried onto the bed, hugging and kissing Mommy and Daddy and getting Christmas tickles. "Okay, let's see if Santa left you two hoodlums anything," Sean told them.

The excitement was one that one would expect from Nichole, now five, and Lauren, now four. They tore the colorful wrapping paper off their gifts and scattered it all over the place. It was a wonderful and joyous Christmas morning for the entire family.

That evening, when the kids were finally in bed and asleep, Sean said, "Hey, Kathryn, lookie here. I think Santa left an envelope with your name on it."

Smiling, Kathryn said, "Oh, did he?" With almost as much enthusiasm as the kids had displayed, Kathryn opened the envelope to see a Ritz Carlton, Naples, Florida, letterhead that showed a hotel confirmation for the first week in January. "Oh, Sean!" she cried out. "Are you kidding?"

Ransom By Mail

"No. I told you I was getting a good bonus, plus I got the corporate deal on the hotel, so it's not as pricy as it normally would be. Merry Christmas, honey."

Kathryn put her arms around her husband and mashed her lips right onto his. As they parted lips, she said, "Thank you! You're the best."

"Come on." Sean pulled Kathryn by the hand. "Let's go to the bedroom, where you can remind me of what you just said."

"We'll see," Kathryn said with a girlish chuckle.

Chapter Sixty-One
The Winslows Celebrate New Year's Eve

New Year's Eve was on a Friday night. The Winslows, desperate to put the prior year of hell behind them and grateful to have their son back, decided to spend a quiet night at home. As baby Ryan slept, Jim and Molly sat in the living room, each with a glass of Champagne, waiting for the ball to drop on Times Square.

With the countdown and the drop of the ball, Molly and Jim toasted the New Year, placed their glasses on the table, embraced, and engaged in a long, passionate kiss.

Jim said, "I love you, Molly."

"I love you too, very much, Jim. Thank you for holding me together this past summer. I couldn't have made it without you."

Jim leaned in for another kiss. After the kiss he grabbed the Champagne glasses, gave one to Molly, and said, "Here's to you, me, and Ryan."

With a big smile, Molly said, "Here, here." They clinked their glasses and drank down the remainder of the Champagne.

Chapter Sixty-Two
The Murphys Celebrate New Year's Eve

At the Murphy household, Jim and Kathryn also were spending a quite night at home, also watching TV and waiting for the ball to drop on Times Square. When the ball dropped, Sean and Kathryn toasted the great year they'd had. The kids were all fine, and they'd had the best summer anyone could imagine. Caring for Nancy's baby, Ryan, had been a joy, and it was great to have received a nice Christmas card from Nancy saying that all was going well for her and Ryan and thanking the two of them for their help the prior summer. Sean's job at ZAP also seemed to be going well. After all, he did get that nice "bonus." Now they toasted with wishes for another great year to come and hoped all would be well.

While getting ready for bed, Kathryn said, "Tomorrow we'll be packing for our trip."

"Yeah, I guess we'd better bring some clothes," Sean said. "Either that or more sun block."

"You're goofy."

"You'll be saying, 'Sean, what the hell are you doing?' I'll say, 'Hell, I can put my sun block on as fast as I want.'"

"There—see?" Kathryn was laughing. "You *are* goofy."

"Yeah, and Happy New Year." Sean grinned as he turned off the lights and squeezed up tight to Kathryn.

Chapter Sixty-Three
The Ritz

The flight from Philadelphia to Fort Lauderdale was quick, with the girls spending most of the time looking out the windows and coloring. After the flight, Sean rented a minivan with a DVD player in the back for the girls to watch while they drove across the state on I-75 through the Everglades to Naples.

The drive was beautiful, with Kathryn asking Sean to stop a couple of times so she could take photographs of the critters and birds in the Everglades along the way.

"God, this warm weather feels so good," she said.

When they arrived at the Ritz Carlton, Kathryn was taken aback by the hotel's elegance. Enormous palm trees framed the tall columns that led into the hotel's main entrance. As they entered the lobby, Kathryn was blown away again with its opulence. "Holy crap, Sean," she whispered. "Can we really afford this?"

Sean grinned. "Yeah, I told you we received a corporate discount, so relax. We won't have to do kitchen work to pay for our bill. Let's enjoy our vacation."

"Oh, my," Kathryn exclaimed as they walked farther into the lobby to see its marble tiled floors, white marble columns, and the gorgeous water fountain in the center.

Kathryn scrambled in her purse, looking for change to give to the girls to toss into the fountain for a wish. The girls already had scurried ahead to the fountain and were eagerly waiting for their parents.

Sean said, "Stay with the girls and I'll check in."

When they got to their room on the sixth floor, Kathryn couldn't believe the ocean view and the pool area. "I feel like a millionaire," she said with a giggle.

Sean just smiled.

Chapter Sixty-Four
It's Baby Ryan

With the weather cooperating, each day at the Ritz seemed better than the last. Every day was a combination of the beautiful beach and pool, with the girls having the time of their lives. Sean and Kathryn also were having a great time relaxing, watching the girls play, and soaking up the sun. The nights were also fantastic. On two of the evenings, Sean had arranged for a sitter through the hotel to watch the children while he and Kathryn went out for dinner and a night on the town, which included Kathryn's favorite pastime, dancing.

This is great, Sean thought. *This is just what I wanted—to have that little extra to make our life's journey much more enjoyable.*

Saturday morning came with Kathryn grumbling, "Oh, crap. Our last day in paradise."

At breakfast, Nichole said she wanted to go to the pool first thing to show off how she could jump into the big pool from the side. She said she wanted her father to catch her after she jumped in. Sean said he couldn't wait to see her jump.

As the family made their way to the large kiddy pool, Kathryn said, "Oh, honey! I forgot the sun block. Could you go into the hotel store and pick up a tube of number forty-five?"

"Sure," Sean said. "I'll be right back."

While he was in the hotel buying sun block for the girls, a couple came walking into the pool area. The wife was pushing a stroller, and a baby boy sat comfortably inside it. As they neared the baby pool, Nichole looked at the woman and shouted, "It's Ryan, Mommy! It's Ryan."

Nichole rushed over to the baby and said, "Hi, Ryan," as she leaned into the stroller and gave the smiling baby a hug. Lauren was quick to follow, standing directly behind her sister, jumping up and down excitedly.

The mother of the baby in the stroller, Molly Winslow, was a bit confused. She couldn't recall Ryan playing with these two girls yesterday at the pool, but apparently they must have as the little girls surely knew Ryan, and he sure as heck was excited to see them.

As Ryan was being unbuckled from the stroller, Kathryn made her way over to her girls and to the baby's mother.

"Hi," Kathryn said. "You must be Nancy. I'm Kathryn, Sean's wife."

Molly was again confused. Jim Winslow was heading over to the women, dragging two pool chairs behind him.

Molly said, "No. I'm sorry. I'm Molly Winslow. This is my husband, Jim."

"Oh, I'm sorry," said Kathryn. "Your baby looks so much like my husband's cousin's baby. We watched him this summer, and he looks so much like your little boy."

Jim's stomach instantly wrenched. "I didn't catch your name..."

"I'm Kathryn Murphy. These are my two daughters, Nichole and Lauren. My husband, Sean, is inside getting us some sun block. He should be right back."

Jim said, "Does your husband work for a pharmaceutical company?"

"Yes," Kathryn said. "Do you know him?"

Jim said, "Yes, I believe so. We played golf with Dr. Tate at Watuppa Country Club."

"That doesn't surprise me," Kathryn said. "I sometimes think Sean spends most of his work time on a golf course. He'll sure be surprised to see you."

"I'm sure he will," Jim said. "Excuse me a moment, please. I have to make a phone call."

Everything was clear as a bell to Jim. Sean Murphy was the dirty bastard who had kidnapped his son and had used his wife and kids to take care of him. Jim pondered the situation for a moment and turned to Molly. "Molly, can I talk with you for a minute?"

Molly looked to Kathryn and asked if she wouldn't mind watching the baby for a moment. Kathryn replied, "Sure, no problem."

Jim led Molly a few feet away, just far enough not to be overheard but still close enough to watch the baby with Kathryn and her kids. "Honey, that woman's husband, Sean, is the son of a bitch who kidnapped our son."

Molly felt lightheaded. "Oh, my God. Are you sure?"

"Yes," said Jim firmly.

"What are you going to do?"

"I'm going to call the authorities. You go back to the baby, and I'll go to the other side of the pool and wait."

As Molly walked back to the baby, Sean came walking out from the hotel holding a bottle of water and a tube of sunscreen. As he headed over to the kiddy pool, he looked over at Molly with her big bonnet hat and sunglasses, not recognizing her.

Kathryn said, "Sean, guess who's here. Jim and Molly Winslow. He said you played golf with him and Dr. Tate."

Sean felt his heart drop directly into his stomach, and an awful feeling of nausea came over him. Kathryn cheerfully said, "Doesn't their baby look just like Nancy's boy?"

Sean stood silently for a moment and didn't notice Jim Winslow standing beside him. Jim leaned close to Sean's ear and said, "Quite a striking resemblance, eh, Sean?"

Without looking back at Jim, Sean dropped straight to his knees next to Kathryn's lounge chair, placed his head on the armrest, and began to sob.

Kathryn was confused. "Sean, what's wrong? What's wrong?" Sean didn't move from his position of despair. He kept his head down and continued to cry.

Jim said, "I'm sorry, Mrs. Murphy, but the baby you cared for this summer was our baby, Ryan, who was kidnapped. Your husband, Sean, kidnapped our baby."

"Oh, Sean!" Kathryn's eyes welled up, and tears began to fall. "Sean, what have you done? Please tell me it's not true."

Sean, his butt now on the concrete and his head on the chair, continued to cry. His life as he knew it, and the lives of his family, were over.

Molly Winslow was holding Ryan. She said, "I'm sorry, Kathryn" then turned and walked away.

Chapter Sixty-Five
I'm Sorry

Nichole and Lauren came out of the kiddy pool, dripping wet, and stood close to Kathryn, asking what was wrong with Daddy. Without answering, Kathryn took her hand from Sean's arm and pulled both girls into her arms. With tears running down her cheeks, she said, "It's okay, girls. Daddy's not feeling well."

Jim leaned over to Sean and said quietly but fiercely, "I should kill you right here, you son of a bitch. But for the sake of your wife and children, we'll do this quietly. Now get up."

Sean didn't resist as Jim held on to his arm, pulling him up. Sean turned to Kathryn, who was still holding the girls, and said, "Honey, I'm so sorry." With that, Jim applied more pressure on his grip and pulled Sean away.

Jim walked Sean directly to the hotel manager's office, where he had Sean sit down to wait for the authorities. Jim quickly explained the situation to the hotel manager and told him the police were on their way.

Sean sat in the chair, his elbows on his knees and his head in his hands. No restraints were necessary; his guilt and shame kept him in place. Jim, however, stood vigil over him, standing a step or two away. The hotel manager called the police and asked them to please have the responding officers come directly to his office without too much commotion so as to not upset any of the hotel's guests.

As the manager hung up the phone, Sean picked up his head and looked up at Jim Winslow. He said, "Jim, I'm sorry."

Jim's patience and control evaporated with that comment. He took a half-step toward Sean, swinging his fist squarely into the side of Sean's head and knocking him out of the chair. As he fell to the floor, Jim kicked him in the gut. "You dirty, rotten bastard." Sean curled into a fetal position with Jim ready to kick him again, but the hotel manager grabbed Jim by the arm and pulled him back just far enough so he couldn't kick Sean again.

"Okay, okay, Mr. Winslow," said the manager. "The police will be here in a moment. Please, please settle down."

Without another word, Jim moved away from the hotel manager, took a seat near the door, and stared directly at Sean.

The hotel manager helped Sean up from the floor and back into the chair. Sean didn't say another word. He sat in the chair and held the side of his face where Jim had slugged him. Even with Sean's head hung low, Jim could see the right side of Sean's face swelling up. It was probably a good thing the hotel manager was there to stop Jim from continuing to beat Sean, because as mad and angry as Jim was, he easily could have killed him right there.

Less than a minute later, two plainclothes policemen arrived with one uniformed cop. The officers cuffed Sean's hands behind his back and took him out of the office and down to the police station. Jim gave one of them his statement about what Sean had done, along with FBI Special Agent Lacher's cell phone number to call and verify his story.

Outside the hotel manager's office, in the hallway, Kathryn stood, holding Lauren on her hip and Nichole by the hand, talking to one of the policemen. The officer was being very sympathetic to Mrs. Murphy and said he would stay with her until she could change into some street clothes and get the girls a sitter from the hotel.

Jim left the hotel with one of the officers to go down to the Naples police station to file the charges and complete the necessary paperwork.

Chapter Sixty-Six
Naples Jail

At the Naples police station, Sean was placed in a temporary holding cell. After he was booked and photographed, he was taken to another cell in the main building. Sean was the only person being held there that day and was told that a little later he would be able to see his wife and call an attorney. Sean humbly thanked the policeman and sat down on the cell bunk.

He was in deep thought and very depressed, thinking about how his life was now completely over and his family's life never would be the same. Kathryn's husband, and Nichole and Lauren's father, was a terrible, wicked person and criminal who had kidnapped a baby. *Shit*, he thought. *How can I face Kathryn? Oh, man, have I screwed things up. What a fucking dickhead asshole I am. I can't believe this happened. What the fuck do I do now?*

In grief and despair, Sean felt the best thing he could do for them now was to be out of their lives completely. No long, drawn-out trial; no prison; no visitations—nothing. *It would be much better for them all if I were dead*, he thought. *Dead. Yes, dead*, he thought, *and that's what I'm going to do right now.*

Sean stood up from his cell bunk and took off the prison jumpsuit they had issued him. He used the pant leg, double tying it to the top of the jail cell door, which was made with old-style steel bars. He twisted the other pant leg up, pulling himself up and facing the door. He was a couple of feet off the floor. With one hand holding the twisted pant leg, he used his free hand to wrap the rest of the other pant leg around his neck. There wasn't any room left for a knot, but if the pant leg were tucked under itself, the weight of his body would cinch it tight. With all his strength holding him off the ground, Sean tucked the rest of the pant leg under the portion of the pant that was around his neck. When it seemed secure, he simply eased his grip and let go. As he had expected, the noose held and slowly began to choke him, depriving his lungs of oxygen. The urge to struggle was there, but Sean fought it, letting his body go limp as he quickly went faint.

Moments later he slipped into unconsciousness and slowly passed from this Earth. By the time the officer had come back to check on him, he was gone.

Chapter Sixty-Seven
Sean

Later on, some people would say Sean was a self-centered, selfish, cowardly person for what he had done and for taking the easy way out. Others would agree that he certainly was a selfish and thoughtless bastard, but all agreed it was probably better for him to be gone and out of the picture so that his family could move on.

Kathryn didn't care what others thought. She had loved Sean deeply, and although she knew what he had done was terribly wrong, she couldn't let go of her image of his kind, gentle, and loving side. This was Kathryn's good and caring nature—the same nature that Sean had deceived and taken advantage of.

Epilogue

The ordeal of Sean's suicide and heinous crime was terrible for poor Kathryn. She had so much to think about and many hard decisions to make, along with two small girls to look after. Despite her loss and harbored feelings, however, life had to move on.

Kathryn's mother took a train with all her pets from California to stay with Kathryn and the girls for a bit. It certainly was a help for Kathryn, but after a while, her mother had to get back to her life in California. She offered to have Kathryn and the girls come live with her, but Kathryn said, "No, thanks, Mom. I really appreciate it and love you for it, but no." She would stay in Pennsylvania where she had her small comfort zone until she could decide what was best for her and the girls.

Sean's employer, ZAP, was more than fair with Sean's final compensation package. The Murphys had some savings, so fortunately Kathryn had some time to sort things out before making any new life changes.

Several months had gone by, and back in New York, Molly was giving her son a bath. She thought about Kathryn and how she probably had given Ryan many baths, changed his diapers, fed him, and given him plenty of caring love. She thought about how horrible it must have been for her to have her whole life destroyed and her heart torn apart. Molly felt awful about this, as she too had experienced a similar loss and sorrow when she had lost Ryan. As soon as Ryan was finished with his bath, Molly picked up the phone, dialed information, and called Kathryn's home. She wanted to reach out to her, as they had somewhat of a common bond. Although it seemed very weird to her for doing it, Molly couldn't let it go and felt it was the right thing to do.

The phone rang, and Kathryn answered.

"Hi," said Molly. "Is this Kathryn?"

"Yes."

"Hi, Kathryn. This is Molly Winslow." Molly paused then said, "May I speak with you?"

For a moment, Kathryn didn't say anything then finally asked, "What do you want to talk about?"

Molly gently replied, "I'm not sure, Kathryn. I just feel we both need to talk to someone."

Kathryn hesitated before wanting to commit, but she too had some questions for which she wanted answers. She said, "Okay." With that the women set up a date for the next day for lunch at Kathryn's house.

That night, Molly told Jim that she had called Kathryn and was going to visit with her. Jim's face took on a blank look. "Please, no," he said. "Just let her be."

Molly became more forceful. "This poor lady watched over our son, loving him and caring for him. She had a wonderful life, and then something went afoul with her husband. It's devastated her life. Do you remember what that felt like?"

"I do," Jim said, "but shouldn't we just let her family be there for her and not interfere?"

"From what I've heard, she only has her mother, who lives out of state. It's only her and the two little girls"

Jim sat down and looked up at his wife. "Okay. I sort of understand, but please be careful of what you get yourself into."

"I hear what you're saying. I just feel it's the right thing to do."

At eleven thirty the next morning, Kathryn and the girls answered the knock on the door. The girls' eyes lit up when they saw Ryan. He was now two and a real pistol of a little boy. Kathryn suggested the girls take Ryan into the family room to play, leaving Molly and Kathryn some private time to talk. When they got to the kitchen, Molly hung her purse on the back of a chair and turned to look at Kathryn, whose eyes were glazed over with puddles ready to burst. As Molly moved to hug Kathryn, they both said they were sorry.

They stayed there, holding each other firmly, letting the feelings and emotions pass through. They felt a true bond—a bond between two women who'd had their lives ripped open and turned upside down. Each knew that no one else would be able to understand this the way they did at that moment.

When the two slowly separated and wiped away their tears, Kathryn said, "Can I get you something to drink? Coffee, tea, water?"

Molly nodded. "That would be great. Tea, please. Can I help?"

The hours and the box of tissues in the kitchen that afternoon were the foundation of a friendship that would last a lifetime. The wounds were now healing, with only small scars showing. Those scars were only visible to those who knew where to look, but the folks who knew where to look weren't looking.

Acknowledgments

I am thankful to my cousin, Donald Payton, who wrote the wonderful book *Friends Are Thicker Than Water: Tales of a Misspent Youth*, which gave me the push I needed to finish my book.

To my good hunting buddy and retired NYPD chief Michael Scagnelli—thanks for the information concerning the police and FBI.

To another good hunting buddy, Kevin Malone, who also wrote a very fascinating book, *Don't Try This at Home*—thanks for the advice.

To Dr. Rick Jackson and his wife, Barbra—thank you for taking the time to give the book a good going over. I hadn't seen that many red pen marks since high school.

I am grateful, as always, to my anchor in life, my loving wife, Cris, who is my go-to girl for everything, including this book. Thanks, toots!

Finally I'd like to thank the Payton family: my mother, Marie; my father, Joseph; my uncles, Martin, Leo, Jim, Johnny, and Eddie; and my dear Aunt May and her husband, Francis Murphy. These folks taught and gave the next generation of Paytons our solid foundations in life, our Irish heritage, and the special gift of telling a good story.

About the Author

Born in the old textile mill town of Fall River, Massachusetts, Paul R. Payton moved to the country when he was twenty-five years old. He became an outdoor enthusiast and wrote numerous articles, detailing his global outdoor adventures, for sportsmen's magazines. His love of the outdoors eventually took him to rural Southeast Nebraska, where he began Sheah Blue Vineyards, which he named after two of his granddaughters. Payton's life in this rural setting of the Midwest was the inspiration for his first novel, *Ransom by Mail*. He recently celebrated his thirty-fifth wedding anniversary with his wife, Cris. They have three children, Sean, Kathryn, and Ryan, and three grandchildren, Blue, Sheah, and Mazlynn.

Made in United States
Orlando, FL
01 November 2023

38481917R00100